WOLF DECIDED

ENSNARED BY THE PACK: BOOK 5

TESSA COLE

Gryphon's Gate Publishing

Wolf Decided

Gryphon's Gate Publishing

550 King St. N.

PO Box 42088 Conestoga

Waterloo, ON

N2L 6K5

Print ISBN: 978-1-990587-24-5

AUDREY

BISHOP RELEASED A STRANGLED GROAN AND CONVULSED, his violent thrashing threatening my grip under his shoulders, but I clenched tighter to his shirt, ignoring the pain in my hands and my trembling arms.

I just had to hold on a little longer, drag him a little farther, find help.

I heaved with all my might, inching closer and closer to the festival, desperate to reach someone, anyone.

Surely someone would notice us. They had to.

But the festival was still going strong even into the early hours of the morning, and while I could hear the dance music and the roar of many voices getting louder, indicating that I was getting closer, the square was on a side street from the main road we were on and a few buildings down.

No one in the square would be able to see us until we'd reached the intersection.

The black and red veins on Bishop's neck and face from the poison — it *had* to be poison because poisons had antidotes — stood out stark against his too-pale skin, and blood poured from his many wounds, leaving thick dark streaks on the ground that shimmered wetly in the moonlight of the realm's two moons.

He wasn't healing.

Not even a little bit.

He should have been healing. A wolf shifter's claws weren't that long, he should have only been seriously bleeding from the gashes in his side, but blood still leaked from his ruined chest.

"Help!" I screamed, my pulse pounding, tears burning my eyes, even as I pushed forward, determined to save him, determined to not be useless when he needed me the most.

I'd just had the most amazing day, and Bishop — gorgeous, wonderful, amazing Bishop — had just told me he loved me. Everything had been perfect and then that man had jumped out of nowhere and dug all his claws into Bishop's chest.

More black and red veins appeared on his neck and cheeks and oozed down his arms and across the back of his hands.

My panic surged, stealing my breath, as something deep within me screamed in agony at the thought of losing Bishop. He was mine. Mine! He couldn't die. I wouldn't let him.

"Help!" *Oh, God, please.* "Help!"

Someone had to know what was going on with him whether he'd been poisoned or enspelled or cursed.

And someone had to save him because I couldn't.

I couldn't shift into my wolf form and mentally call for help, and even if I did somehow have telepathy, I wouldn't be able to use it in my human form like the shifters in this realm could. That just wasn't possible for shifters from my realm.

A wave of panic crashed through me, sudden and ferocious, stealing my breath and threatening to bring me to my knees.

Knox.

Knox could feel my fear through our mating bond.

And through his twin bond with Bishop, he could feel his brother dying.

Another sob caught in my throat. There were too many emotions rushing through me, overwhelming me, and on the verge of ripping me apart. I could barely catch my breath. It was too much, too—

Audrey. I'm coming, Knox said in my head, sending a wave of love and determination through our bond. But my fear was too strong, and I couldn't stop that horrible voice in my head that said I was going to fail Bishop and Knox because I wasn't strong enough.

Because I was useless.

No, I mentally screamed back at the voice. Those thoughts weren't mine. They were Merrick's and Sterling's, beaten into me for years. I was weak. I was useless. No one wanted me.

But Bishop had proven that wasn't true.

He wanted me for me and not because of a mating bond or anything else. He'd seen me at my worst and still told me he loved me.

And I was God damned going to save him, even if all I could do was drag him down the road to someone who could help him.

Knox in his enormous black wolf form raced out of the shadows of a side street, sending a flicker of relief snapping through me. *He* could call for help. Hell, *he* probably knew where the closest med pack was.

He shifted into his human form and took Bishop from me, lifting him into his arms as if he didn't weigh anything, because, of course, with his shifter strength Bishop's weight was nothing.

"What happened?" he asked, picking up his pace and heading to the building on the corner of the intersection.

"Some guy attacked us."

A chill raced down my spine. Bishop had shoved me out of the way. I'd been right in the attacker's path, and once I was out of the way, the guy kept trying to get past Bishop to get to me.

"No," I said, unable to keep the trembling from my voice at the realization that the poison or whatever was killing Bishop had been meant for me. "Some guy attacked *me.*"

And Bishop had paid the price.

Cyrus and Nova raced into sight, Nova heading into

the building on the corner while Cyrus stormed toward us.

"What happened?" he snarled, making my pulse pick up with a different fear.

Was he going to blame me for Bishop? If I hadn't wanted to go to the festival. If I hadn't danced for as long or as short as I had. If I hadn't been foolish enough to think I could fit into this pack, be mated to Knox, and also have Bishop court me without consequences none of this would have happened.

But it didn't matter what Cyrus thought or did to me if Bishop didn't make it. None of this would matter. I could already feel my heart and soul starting to crack and knew I'd forever be incomplete without him.

Which didn't make sense. He wasn't my mate yet. We hadn't taken the vows and sealed the bond. I shouldn't be feeling as if I was losing my bonded mate, which only made me worry about how bad it would be if something happened to Knox.

"Set him down," Nova commanded as she hurried out of the house with a bright yellow duffle bag.

Knox lay Bishop on the ground and grabbed my hand, yanking me to his side before taking one of Bishop's hands while Nova went to work. His fear and anger and desperation churned in my stomach and I could feel him barely holding his wolf back.

I was losing him, too.

God, this wasn't happening.

But Knox's and Bishop's twin bond was unusually

strong. They could sense each other's emotions just like those in a mating bond, and I had no doubt if one of them died, the other would suffer as if they'd lost a bonded mate.

Which meant Knox would go crazy, most likely going feral, or he'd die.

Fear gripped my heart at the thought while something deep inside me, something hard and angry and wild, whispered in my soul.

Neither of them were dying or going crazy. I wouldn't allow it.

They were mine.

AUDREY

I SENT AS MUCH LOVE AND STRENGTH THROUGH THE MATING bond as I could, determined to anchor Knox in his body so his wolf wouldn't take over and go feral. Then I grabbed a handful of gauze from the med pack ready to get to work because there was no way I was going to just sit there and cry when I could do something to help.

Nova tore open Bishop's shirt and my pulse lurched, my breath stalling in my throat and cold dread flash-freezing around my heart.

There was so much blood. It coated his chest and side and pooled on the road around his body while more red and black veins covered his chest in a thick web.

"Fuck," Cyrus snarled his power rolling over me, making me tremble but thankfully not forcing me to do anything because I didn't have time to grovel.

I was going to save my mate... or rather, my soon-to-be mate.

I mentally shoved at Cyrus's power and pressed my handful of gauze against Bishop's side, trying to staunch the blood from eight deep gashes, but my hands weren't big enough to cover them all.

"Knox," Nova said, jerking her chin toward me, and he dropped Bishop's hand and took over with his much larger hands.

"What the fuck is that?" Cyrus dropped to his knees beside Nova and was about to reach into the med pack when Bishop gasped a sharp breath, his only warning, before screaming and convulsing.

I shoved my hands under his head as it slammed down on the road, sending agony racing through my fingers before Cyrus took over from me.

"If the streaks were all red and a fraction of the size, I'd say it's *karoose* venom," Nova said, popping off the stoppers on the med pack's two elixirs then pouring both of them into Bishop's mouth the second he stopped convulsing. "We need Whil."

"Right here," the summer fae called out as she hurried around the corner from the side street, looking like the perfect fairy tale image of a fae from Fairy.

She, like all fae, was stunning and ageless, and her perpetual golden glow shone brightly in the dim light, even with a streetlight nearby, giving her an ethereal, magical presence.

"Have you seen anything like this?" Nova asked as Cyrus handed me more gauze and together we applied pressure to the wounds on Bishop's chest.

"Not since the last of the gods were awake." Whil placed her hands on Bishop's forehead and closed her eyes. "It's *karoose* venom imbued with a god or goddess's power. The healing elixirs will help but not enough to cure him. He needs to be fully submerged in the healing pool so I can pull it out of him."

"We need to get him to the Residence," Cyrus said as Nova ripped off a piece of tape and handed it to him. "Before we draw a crowd."

He, Nova, and Whil all glanced at Knox then went back to taping fresh gauze to Bishop's wounds.

"My wolf is under control," Knox growled even as the turmoil churning through our bond grew stronger. "Bishop needs us."

"Keep it that way," Cyrus replied as he picked up Bishop and raced up the road.

Knox swept me into his arms and followed while Nova stripped, shifted, and raced ahead.

We passed through the open gate to the Residence and ran around the outside of the building until we reached a small, partially sheltered patio in front of a set of French doors that looked a lot like the ones to my suite.

Someone had set out a mattress just like when I'd woken up after Sterling had tricked me into hurting myself, and Cyrus set Bishop on it while Knox, still holding me as if I were the only thing keeping him in his body, sagged to the ground beside him.

"Tell me he at least killed whoever attacked him," Cyrus snapped as Nova rushed out my suite doors wearing a different colored dress than the one she'd left with Whil and carrying her doctor's bag.

She dropped beside Bishop and pulled out a stitching kit as Whil hurried to join her with gauze and saline.

"He got away," I stated, my voice steadier than I would have expected given how Cyrus made me nervous. He was a powerful alpha and he'd made his position about me clear. He didn't like me, thought I didn't know my place, and I'd been trying for the last few days to stay small and invisible and not do anything that would upset him.

And now, I didn't care.

Now that wildness inside me whispered to fight for my mate. Fight and win.

"Fuck," he snarled. "Tell me everything." His power roared over me stealing my breath, squeezing my insides, and drawing a whimper even as my wildness demanded I stay strong.

Knox growled low in his throat, the sound more wolf than human even though he was still fully in his human form.

"Fuck," Cyrus barked again and his power vanished, making me shudder with the sudden loss. He raked his hands through his hair pulling strands from the braid that kept his longer hair on top away from his face and shaved sides.

"The man wore thick clothes with a hood so I couldn't see his face or any distinguishing marks," I said before Cyrus could lose control of his power again and because I needed him to send out watchmen and hunters to catch whoever had attacked us.

And while the thought of catching the assailant pissed off the wildness inside me that really wanted him dead, keeping him alive meant we might get answers, like why he'd want to poison me instead of just kill me or where he'd gotten the poison.

"He ran down an alley when it looked like Bishop was going to win their fight, then Bishop collapsed," I added. "He was hurt, but not so bad that he couldn't have shifted out most of his injuries."

Cyrus's eyes narrowed and he pursed his lips, pausing for a moment, hopefully ordering the pack to find whoever it was.

"Okay," he growled a second later, more of his power rippling over me as if he couldn't fully contain it. "The pool is six days away, five if we push it. I'm assuming," he said turning to Whil, "that because you said we need to get him in it, he can last that long."

"But not much longer," Whil said.

"Nova, you and Lucius are in charge. We can't afford to take a whole team, so Deacon is coming with us." He glanced at the moons creeping closer and closer to the western horizon. "Dawn is in a couple of hours. Will that give you enough time to get ready?" he asked, turning his attention back to Whil and making that strange wildness — that, now that I thought about it had to be coming from Knox — rise in anger. It didn't matter that she needed to come. It mattered that Cyrus wasn't asking me as well and I sure as hell was going.

"I only need to pack," I replied as if he'd asked me instead of just Whil.

Cyrus's attention snapped to me, his eyes narrowed, and his power rose, a great wave on the verge of crashing over me and forcing me to submit. "You're not going."

The wildness surged from the depths of my soul, and I met his gaze, directly challenging him. "Yes. I am."

"No." His tenuous control snapped and his power slammed into me, stealing my breath and demanding I look away, bow down, and submit.

Which was *not* happening.

My mates needed me, Bishop because he was dying and Knox because he was barely keeping his wolf from going feral. Cyrus could throw everything he had at me, but I wouldn't give in.

I wouldn't even give in so I could find another way to go, which was what I usually did. Step back, submit, and shut my mouth. That was what I always did and it had kept me alive.

But now there wasn't another way. Not going with them would kill me. Maybe not right away, but if I lost them, I'd wither away to nothing. On top of that, it wasn't safe to follow them from a distance. With their heightened senses, Cyrus would know I was following them and going beyond the town's limits by myself was too dangerous.

Of course, standing my ground now meant Cyrus

could punish me and lock me up, and I'd be trapped in Stonehaven unable to protect my soul's mates.

No. I wouldn't let that happen.

My pulse *thu-thudded*, hard and fast, and I fought to breathe against the pressure.

"I'm going," I insisted as another wave of Cyrus's power slammed into me.

My body started to bow, submitting to his will, as my soul screamed in fear and fury.

"No," I gritted out, straightening my back with another *thu-thud*, making Cyrus's eyes widen and his power flare stronger.

"Back the fuck off," Knox snapped, his own power adding to the crushing mix.

"It's too dangerous," Cyrus snarled back.

The devastating force I'd felt outside the death god's temple when Cyrus had made Knox submit crackled in the air and seized my muscles.

"I'm. Going."

My pulse roared, pounding hard, surging strength to my limbs, and I heaved to my feet, squared my shoulders, and glared into Cyrus's now shocked expression.

"Mine," I snarled at him, my voice sounding strange and gravelly. "I won't leave my mates when they need me and you can't make me."

CYRUS

AUDREY'S GAZE DRILLED INTO MINE IN A FIERCE CHALLENGE. Somehow, she'd resisted my power and even had the strength to stand, completely defying my command. If I hadn't felt the ferocious force pouring off her, I'd have no idea how she'd done it.

Hell, I still didn't. I had no idea where the power had come from.

Sure, her bond with Knox was unusually strong, but that wouldn't have allowed her to channel his power. And besides, I could feel Knox's radiating from him, so he obviously wasn't giving it to Audrey.

No. This alpha power was all hers. A glimpse deep into her soul at what her ancestors had locked away with a curse.

It had only taken her bonded mate to be on the verge of going feral and her soon-to-be mate dying for it to make an appearance.

Except as soon as I thought that I knew it was wrong. She and Bishop might not have had a mating bond or even just a bonding ceremony publicly announcing their love for each other, but they were mates.

At the disastrous dinner a week ago, Bishop had said Audrey and Knox were fated for each other. It had been an easier way to explain what had happened than saying Audrey had already started a mating bond with someone else and when we'd found her close to death that bond had connected with Knox's soul.

But now I wondered if it hadn't actually been the truth. She'd brought Knox back from being feral and was now helping him hold off his panic so he could stay in control and protect his brother.

Bishop had told me the other day that Knox had been more relaxed in the one full day of being with Audrey before he'd had to leave on a hunt than he'd ever been — and more like the brother I'd known before his claustro-phobia had gotten out of control.

Knox had needed to have the scare of his life when he thought she was going to die, but it had broken through the rest of his resistance to a mate he hadn't wanted and had actually been good for him. Before this attack, he'd seemed genuinely happy.

Bishop had been happy, too. Happier than I'd seen him in a long while. He'd practically glowed with happi-ness every time I'd gotten a glimpse of him and Audrey wandering around the festival, and he hadn't hesitated to be affectionate with her while the rest of the pack watched.

Hell, he'd sung her *Fated Stars* at the dance, which was Bishop's way of publicly announcing Audrey was the woman he'd been searching for.

He and Audrey were fated for each other, too. Their mating bond had probably already started to form even though neither of them had said the vows to awaken the magic that bound their souls together.

And it completely explained why Audrey was willing to defy me to stay with them and why the wolf locked deep in her soul was suddenly stronger than her curse. Bonded mates would do anything to protect each other.

"Nova," Audrey said, refusing to look away from me. "Do you still need my help or can I go pack?"

"I'm good," Nova replied, her voice strained with all the alpha power crashing around us which was another surprise. Normally she would have told me to grow up and pull it back so she could work, but she'd remained silent.

Was she too stunned to see that Audrey's power held its own against mine or had she wanted to give Audrey the chance to stand up for herself?

Probably a combination of both. Audrey had only stood up to me once and that was to defend her actions when she'd risked her life to save a group of children from a grimalkin.

My wolf had howled with joy at her defiance, falling even more in love with her. She was everything we'd been waiting for. She could challenge us and stand at our side in battle. She would be the mother of our pups because she was ours.

But even as I glared at her, I could feel her power trembling. She wasn't fully aware of it or her wolf, and the effort it took to push past the curse was taking its toll on her body. Not to mention the emotional toll of defying everything that had been beaten into her during her childhood along with her naturally gentle disposition.

She was holding on by her all-too-human fingernails and could lose it at any second, destroying everything she'd just shown me.

"Alpha," she spat out in acknowledgment before squeezing Knox's shoulder and marching into her suite.

"You were saying, *alpha?*" Nova said, her tone dry.

I glared at her. "Don't start. It's dangerous on the road to Savaria and it'll be even more dangerous when we leave the road to get to the pool."

"It's dangerous here," Knox growled. "That man didn't attack Bishop. He went after Audrey. Bishop was hurt defending her."

Fuck.

Her shirt had been torn open, but I hadn't thought anything about it. She hadn't been acting as if she were hurt. I'd assumed all the blood on her was Bishop's.

"We need to check her," I said as my wolf lurched against my hold. It didn't care how pissed off she was at us. He had to protect her and he couldn't stand the idea of losing both her and Bishop.

"She hasn't been poisoned," Knox replied, his tone barely human.

"Maybe she was nicked or only inhaled a bit of it and it isn't spreading as fast." Sisters, I had to protect her. Save her. Now now now. "You might not be able to tell with your bond with Bishop going crazy."

"If I was losing them both, I'd be feral," Knox replied. "If you want to keep it that way, she'll stay with me."

"I could also use the help," Whil added. "I can keep Bishop alive without Nova's help, but a second set of hands would be helpful. Especially if we run into trouble."

"You don't need to convince me," I ground out, my insides churning. I needed to stay in control of myself and this situation, needed to make sure everyone was safe and survived this poison.

Still, I really didn't want Audrey to go with us. We might not be traveling through the northern wilderness, but everything within me screamed that it was still too dangerous, especially with Bishop unconscious and Knox barely holding it together.

I wouldn't be able to protect her the way she deserved... the way I *had* to protect her.

Except I also couldn't leave her here.

"We don't know who attacked them," I said, "so she's safest with us." With me.

I wanted to say it was a foreigner who'd attacked her and Bishop and that she'd be safe with the pack, but without Bishop to identify the culprit's scent, I couldn't assume anything. Which made my wolf even more determined to keep her close and the rest of me furious.

Were there members of my pack who were so determined to get rid of her they'd kill her? And why use poison? She wouldn't survive against any of us in our wolf form. Why not just attack her and be done with it?

I'd thought with her being noticeably nervous and submissive around me that the rumors that I was interested in Audrey would finally die, but it looked like that was a serious miscalculation.

Bishop moaned and his muscles tightened but he didn't convulse, the elixir thankfully easing the worst of the poison's effects.

Maybe I wasn't the reason Audrey had been targeted. Even before Bishop had proclaimed Audrey his soon-to-be mate, he'd showered her with affection and made no attempt to hide it.

Not that he should. Bishop could mate whoever he wanted, not like—

My thoughts stuttered. I'd been holding my wolf back from pursuing her because she was weak and I didn't think the pack would respect her if we mated.

But now she'd revealed an enormous power strong enough to challenge me and possibly win.

Of course, she was still cursed and once her adrenaline wore off, she'd be back to being a powerless shifter.

Was that how it was always going to be with her or was there a way to completely break the curse?

She'd gained strength with strong emotions, like

when she'd defended her decision to sacrifice herself to save those kids, and now with her determination to stay with her mates.

If I pushed her, would I be able to get her to break through and permanently become the shifter she'd just shown me?

"Whatever you're thinking," Nova said with her uncanny ability to know when I was thinking something stupid regarding a woman. "Stop. Just stop."

And she was right. The last time I'd pushed Audrey, she'd withdrawn into herself and become so submissive it made me want to scream.

Still, there had to be a way to help her without destroying her... because I needed her at my side just like she was at my brothers' sides.

I didn't care if she was strong or not, but I didn't want to put her in a situation where my pack constantly questioned her worth or where our mating created challenges to my leadership.

I already knew how she'd take that and it wouldn't be with anger. She'd get withdrawn and submissive again and feel guilty even though it wasn't her fault.

Fuck.

This was a no win situation.

And I couldn't keep standing here. I had to meet with Lucius and Deacon, arrange for a cart to be ready at the north gate, and get someone to put supplies together for Bishop and Knox — since neither of them were in any shape to do their own packing.

Without thinking, I jerked open the doors leading to Audrey's suite and stormed inside. It was the fastest way to get to my office so I could meet with my betas and get everything done in the next two hours that needed to get done.

But the second the door closed I was surrounded by her scent, soft and sweet and soured by fear, making my wolf growl with anger. Then a small hiccupping sob sounded from the bedroom and my wolf rushed me to the open bedroom door before I could stop him.

To my horror, Audrey sat on the bed, tears streaming down her cheeks and her hands covering her mouth trying to muffle her sobs. She froze when she saw me, her eyes widening with fear and her body trembling.

Shit.

All her adrenaline was gone, she wasn't radiating a hint of alpha power, and the terror of the night had finally come crashing down on her.

I mentally cursed myself. Given that she could also sense how Knox felt, she was probably experiencing double her usual emotions, and with them so strong, it had to be overwhelming.

On top of that, she'd outwardly defied her alpha and everything she knew told her she couldn't do that, not without repercussions. And now that the moment of determination had passed, all her old fears had returned.

"I don't care what you do to me, but don't make me stay here," she begged, her voice raspy with tears, her reaction to me the complete opposite of what it had been outside. "Punish me after they're saved."

Fucking hell. I wanted angry Audrey back.

But this was just proof that I couldn't continue playing the villain. Not even if it was better for me to keep my distance from her. Just seeing me terrified her and I couldn't take it anymore. This was the last straw.

It had been hard enough to keep my distance from her and pretend I didn't see her so I wouldn't keep scaring her. And it had been even harder today when I'd kept catching glimpses of her wandering around the market with Bishop and couldn't make myself look away.

She'd been shy and uncertain at first, which tore at my heart, but as Bishop got her to relax and she stopped glancing at all the people watching her and just had fun, it was like watching a morning flower open to the first rays of sunshine.

By the time they'd reached the square with the dancing, she'd been radiant, making others around her smile because she was so happy it was contagious. Many of my pack had stopped looking at her like she was dangerous or a strange curiosity and saw the stunning woman I'd seen grow before my very eyes during our journey north.

I wanted radiant Audrey back. Needed her. Not just for myself but for my brothers and the rest of my pack. They needed to remember that strength came in many forms, and gentleness and kindness weren't a weakness, they were what kept a community thriving.

"Audrey." I stepped into the room and she shrunk in

on herself, tugging her ruined shirt closed to hide her body, but I kept going until I was at the edge of the bed, close enough to touch her, then sank to my knees. "I'm sorry. I shouldn't have said the things I said to you."

She blinked, her expression still scared as if she hadn't fully heard me, and I desperately wanted to wrap my arms around her and never let go.

But that would only scare her more.

"I was wrong," I added, praying that she'd heard me. My apology wouldn't make everything right, but hopefully it was a start, the first step in proving that even if she never forgave me, she could say what she wanted and not fear reprisal. "There's no good excuse for why I yelled at you in the arena. I didn't think and I hurt you. I'm so very sorry."

AUDREY

Cyrus's words were a trap. They had to be.

I'd just defied him, challenged his authority by refusing to look away. No one did that to an alpha and got away with it.

Even if I'd only done it in front of his brother and his trusted friends, he still should have been furious with me.

Except he wasn't, and every instinct I had told me he was being sincere, that he meant his apology.

Which didn't help me figure out how to respond. Did I just accept it and pretend nothing had happened?

A minute ago, when I'd been filled with what had to have been Knox's ferocious wildness — since it couldn't have been mine — I would have said yes. But the wildness had vanished the moment I'd stepped inside, and now all I felt was a terrifying, nauseating churn of emotions that were both mine and Knox's along with a bone-deep exhaustion.

In the back of my mind, I knew it was shock. The adrenaline from the fight, trying to save Bishop, and the fight to stay with Knox and Bishop had worn off, and I was crashing. Hard.

I didn't have it in me to figure out how to respond to Cyrus.

"I'll put a pack together for you." He glanced at my wardrobe as if he could look beyond the closed doors and see that after I changed out of my ruined shirt, I wouldn't have a spare. It wasn't my fault my clothes kept getting ruined, but for any other alpha that wouldn't have mattered, and I swore to myself that once I'd made myself a valuable member of the pack, I'd pay Cyrus back. For everything.

I hugged myself tighter and tried to imagine how the wildness had felt rushing through me in a desperate attempt to keep me from getting any more submissive than I already was.

I'd liked feeling powerful, liked feeling as if I had control over my life.

I wanted that feeling back.

I wanted it to stay.

"Change your clothes and shoes," he said, his attention shifting to my feet and the sandals he'd given me when I'd first arrived in his realm. "And get back out there. They both need you, and I want Nova to give you a once over before we head out."

"So if I'm hurt you can order me to stay?" I huffed, the words slipping out on a sudden wave of frustration.

"No." He ran a hand through his hair, mussing it even more and releasing a heavy breath.

For a second, he looked as exhausted as I felt... and as heartbroken.

The urge to hold him, comfort him, and take comfort from his embrace as if he were one of my mates rose inside me like a great wave.

Both his brothers were in danger, and he, an alpha, had just humbled himself to the weakest shifter in existence. Not to mention he had someone running around town wielding a dangerous poison. He didn't just have his brothers or me to worry about. He had the whole pack.

Then his expression snapped back to serious and he stood, startling me and — much to my frustration — making me instinctively shrink back further up the bed.

"Knox and Bishop need you, and you need them," he said. "You're going with us. Whil said she wanted your help keeping Bishop stable, and you now know how to forage, find ideal firewood, and set up a safe fire. Having you along will be helpful."

His expression shifting into something I couldn't recognize, he inched closer as if he wanted to... I had no idea what. Touch me? Hold me?

But then he froze and the muscles in his jaw flexed. "We leave in less than two hours. Try to get some sleep if you can."

With that, he stormed out of my bedroom and, a moment later, I heard the door to my suite, the one leading into the hall and not outside, open and close.

I stared out my bedroom doorway into the sitting room, a heavy confusion swirling into the mix of all my other emotions.

What had just happened?

I was going to be helpful?

I must have hallucinated the whole conversation. I hadn't done anything right in Cyrus's eyes from the very beginning, and now I was going to be helpful?

Also, an alpha just apologized to me. Me! And that made strange, hopeful feelings warm around my heart.

I quickly showered off Bishop's blood, trying hard not to think about how I'd gotten it on me, changed my shirt and pants, replaced my sandals with my hiking boots, and headed back to the private patio outside my suite.

First things first: reassure Knox that I was holding it together. He'd been too caught up with his failing twin bond to register my sobbing breakdown the second I'd entered my suite or my emotions from my strange conversation with Cyrus, and I planned to keep it that way. He had more than enough to worry about.

After that, once we were on our way, I'd ask Whil about the magical block she'd cast on me to keep Sterling out of my head. I couldn't afford to be mistaken about the conversation with Cyrus and didn't want to risk having been manipulated.

Outside, Knox had shifted into his wolf form, the stress of Bishop being near death too much for him, but I could tell he was still himself. His wolf hadn't completely taken over, and he hadn't lost his mind, although I could sense both of them fighting to keep it together. Across from him, Nova was finishing up wrapping Bishop's wounds to keep them clean and Whil was gone, presumably at her cottage packing.

"Cyrus wanted me to give you a quick check," she said. "Now that your adrenaline has worn off, does anything hurt?"

I opened my mouth to say no but made myself pause. Whether the order had come from Cyrus or not, this was a genuine question and it was best to take it seriously just in case I was injured and it got worse halfway to the pool.

My hands hurt from where they'd been caught between Bishop's head and the ground as well as from gripping Bishop's shirt and dragging him down the road, and the rest of me was getting achier and achier by the second from dragging him as well as a full night of dancing. But it wasn't serious, not something worth wasting an elixir on.

My foot, however, hurt a lot more than my hands from when Bishop had convulsed and I'd dropped him.

I didn't think anything was broken, but it was best if Nova looked at it. That, and it would give her something to tell Cyrus when he inevitably asked her about me.

"I'm a little beat up," I told her, showing the bruises that were starting to form on the back of my hands, "but not too bad. My foot got the worst of it."

I took off my boot and more worry bled through my mating bond with Knox as he nudged my arm with his damp nose.

"I think it's just a bad bruise," I added, wrapping my arms around his neck and leaning my head against his.

His rich wood smoke scent enveloped me and the warmth of our bond wrapped around my heart, steadying my soul, while Nova studied my foot.

Please don't let it be broken. Please don't let this be the reason Cyrus refuses to let me go.

I didn't want to fight him again. I still felt shaky and exhausted from standing up to him. And while he'd said I was going and I'd be useful, a broken foot would change everything.

I'd challenge him again if I had to. I could feel that certainty deep in my soul. But then I'd also turn back into a shivering sobbing mess once I'd won.

Except I didn't believe I'd broken down the moment I'd stepped into my suite because I'd challenged Cyrus and was afraid of him. I'd broken down because it was all too much. Bishop had just told me he loved me and was now dying, and the roar of Knox's emotions, his rage and panic and desperation over the thought that he was losing his bonded twin, was threatening to drown me.

I'd been submerged under all that emotion once the adrenaline and wildness had rushed out of me, and it was a miracle I wasn't a sobbing ball of completely-messed-up buried between Knox and Bishop right now.

"It's just a nasty bruise," Nova confirmed, releasing my foot. She'd felt every bone and flexed every joint and now it was really throbbing. "It's starting to swell, so I've asked Eloise to bring you an ice pack. It's going to hurt while you walk for the next few days." Her gaze grew unfocused for a moment then she turned her attention back to me. "I've told Cyrus you need to ride in the cart with Bishop for the next two days. You barely weigh anything as it is, so he and Deacon won't notice you riding along."

"He and Deacon?" I asked, confused.

They'll be taking turns pulling the cart, Knox said.

"Ah." I didn't know what to say about that. It made sense, though. Knox would need to stay in contact with Bishop, and neither Whil nor I were strong enough to pull a cart with a full grown man in it. Also, Cyrus wasn't like my previous alpha... or at least he was somewhat different. He did manual labor and had done chores like everyone else when we'd travel north. It made sense that he'd take turns pulling the cart.

"You can do this, Audrey," Nova said.

She stood and gave me a soft smile as Eloise hurried around the flowering shrub that made the patio private, carrying an ice pack.

"By the Sisters!" she gasped, the sight of Bishop's bandaged body covered in horrible black and red veins making her stumble. Then her attention jumped to me. "Oh, child. He'll be alright. Nova and Whil are miracle workers. They'll save him. I'm sure of it."

She knelt and gently pressed the ice pack against my foot, making tears burn my eyes.

It was such a big thing for her to think of me while one of her pack alphas was gravely ill since no one ever thought of me. No one in my old pack would have cared that my heart was breaking, they'd have only been worried about Bishop.

Knox whined and sent confusion and reassuring love through our bond, not knowing how to take my sudden swell of emotions.

I sent love back to him. "I'm okay. Just—" I met Eloise's eyes. "Thank you."

"Come on, Eloise," Nova said. "They need their rest and we've got rations to make and pack."

"Right." Eloise offered me a smile just as soft and warm as Nova's, sending more warmth radiating around my heart.

Mine, whispered something inside me so quietly I could barely hear it. *My people. My pack. Mine.*

The voice had to have come from Knox because if I even had a wolf, she was buried so deep within me she was never waking up.

Although maybe... just maybe that wasn't completely true anymore.

KNOX

AUDREY SNUGGLED CLOSER TO ME, HELD THE ICE PACK against her bruised foot, and passed out ten minutes later. She'd been amazing. A glorious, determined goddess standing up to Cyrus and asking for what she wanted.

I knew she had alpha power enough to tease mine, but I didn't expect it to be strong enough to fully challenge my brother. She hadn't backed down or looked away once, and I couldn't have been more proud of her and more furious that she felt she had to tear past the curse locking her wolf away to ensure she could stay with her mates.

And given the feelings coming from both Bishop and Audrey, they were mates already. They just needed the bond.

Cyrus had seen that truth even while his power had tried to get her to submit. I'd seen it in his eyes. There wasn't any other reason for Audrey, who'd become far too nervous around him while I was away on a hunt, to defy him. That kind of determination, and that kind of power, only manifested when a mating bond was in danger of being broken, and I'd felt that it hadn't just been our bond she was fighting for.

Which was good and a relief in a way. She'd just demonstrated that she was an extremely powerful female alpha which meant her heat fever might not just have been because we hadn't sealed our bond. Powerful females had powerful heats and often instinctively took multiple mates because of that.

Bishop was her second mate, but she'd probably need at least one more.

And somehow, that idea didn't piss off my wolf. It knew she needed more mates to keep her safe and it was good with anything that protected Audrey.

I shifted into my human form, my wolf having settled enough to allow the change now that Audrey was cuddled against us. I pulled her into my arms and settled against Bishop's side with Audrey between us, and the agony screaming through my twin bond eased a bit, our souls steadying him, reassuring him that we were doing everything in our power to save him.

This. This was how it was supposed to be.

Bishop had been so sure that we'd share a mate, but I hadn't believed him. I couldn't imagine any woman willing to put up with me and all my broken bits.

And yet, here she was, beautiful and kind and smart and perfect.

I'd never felt so comfortable in my human skin before and my wolf had never felt steadier. None of his primal wildness had vanished. In fact, it felt stronger, energized, as if Audrey physically strengthened us, but now all that power was focused on her, protecting her, cherishing her, loving her. Our mate.

She was the one we'd been waiting for our whole life. She was love. She was comfort.

She was home.

And when I found whoever had tried to kill her and poisoned Bishop, I was going to tear him limb from limb. I didn't care if it was a member of our pack or not. Bishop and Audrey were mine, and I protected what was mine.

Somehow, I managed to doze with her, waking when Deacon stepped onto the semi-private patio outside Audrey's suite.

"We're just about ready to go," he said softly, thankfully not waking Audrey since I could still feel her exhaustion radiating through our bond. "How's she holding up?"

My wolf grinned at his question. It meant, unlike some members of the pack, he'd accepted her. While I'd been skulking in the shadows at the festival, daring to get as close as possible to keep an eye on her, I'd heard whispers and seen the dark looks thrown at Bishop and Audrey when their backs were turned.

Not everyone was happy she was in the pack. Most

didn't seem to care that she was my mate, but Bishop was another story. She wasn't good enough for him, wasn't strong enough.

If only they'd seen her challenge Cyrus. If only I could help her wolf fully wake.

But she was just as broken as I was and a lot more fragile. Whether she wanted to or not, she cared about other people, and that meant it hurt her when they were cruel to her. I didn't care. If you were an asshole then I ignored you. Hell, if you were a person, I mostly ignored you. But Audrey didn't want that. She wanted a pack. I think she even needed one to feel fulfilled in her life. She needed to help people.

Bishop was the mate who could give that to her. He could introduce her to the people who could help her satisfy that need.

"She might not look it." And she might not believe it. "But she's tough," I whispered back.

"Oh, I believe it. Did Nova tell the truth?" he asked. "Was she part of that alpha power battle that woke up the entire Residence?"

I stiffened at that. "Who else knows?"

"No one. Nova only told me. Everyone thinks it was you losing your shit over Bishop."

"So they know he's poisoned?" Fuck. Were they going to blame Audrey for that? I didn't understand how people reacted, but I knew people would look for someone to blame and at the moment Audrey was an easy target. She looked like prey in a whole town of predators.

"They knew there was trouble." Deacon's expression turned grim, something that looked so out of place on him it made me sit up, worry rushing through me.

Audrey groaned in her sleep, and I brushed my hand over her head, hoping to soothe her back to sleep. If the pack was blaming Audrey, I didn't want her to hear this conversation. She was already shaken up by the attack and by standing up to Cyrus... something that shouldn't have terrified her but did.

"Tell me," I growled. "Who do I need to protect my mate from?"

"Whoa." He raised his hands and crouched beside me. "Now's not the time to wolf out."

My wolf took over and deepened our growl. "Tell. Me. Why is Audrey afraid of Cyrus? Why did she feel she had to fight him to stay by my and Bishop's side?"

"Cyrus isn't who she has to worry about." Deacon sighed and rolled his eyes, his expression turning wry. "You know how he gets when he isn't in control of the situation."

I narrowed my eyes. I knew all too well that Cyrus would do anything, say anything to protect his pack, and I'd seen him growl at Audrey for the entire walk to the death god's temple. He'd been freaking out over the fact that she had no wilderness skills and that if we got separated, she'd die.

"What did he do?" My fury as well as my wolf's was starting to boil over, and Audrey, while still asleep, somehow knowing I was upset, rolled over and wrapped her arms around me.

My wolf huffed, the warmth of our connection and her love calming some of our anger. We couldn't go on a rampage, no matter how much we wanted to beat the shit out of Cyrus. That would leave Audrey unprotected.

"She really is something, isn't she?" Deacon sighed.

"Don't change the topic."

"Wasn't trying," he said. "Just amazed by your mate. Not even Bishop can calm you like that. She pulled you out of a near-feral state, you know."

"I remember."

"That scared the shit out of Cyrus." Deacon ran a hand over his face making me wonder if he'd gotten any sleep. Yesterday had been the first day of the festival, the day when everyone danced until dawn. "I told him not to, but he lost his temper and yelled at her. I was already taking you up to the sacred grove so I don't know what he said to her, but she turned into a complete mouse, afraid of everyone and everything."

My wolf started growling again, and Audrey nuzzled closer, drawing in a deep breath of my scent, settling him again.

"Nova and I helped Bishop reassure her that she was safe, and I think she was starting to regain her confidence, at least with a few of us, but Finn and Velora are particularly suspicious of her and I suspect they've been spreading rumors." He sighed. "The fact that she was with Bishop when he was attacked—"

"When *she* was attacked," I corrected.

His eyes widened in shock. "She was the target? Fuck. Of course she was. No one has tried to hurt any of you in your life. Audrey is the only thing that's changed."

"I have to keep her safe," I told him. "I won't hesitate to protect her, but that could be bad for her." I could be thrown out of the pack.

If enough people told Cyrus I was dangerous, he'd have no choice but to throw me out or face who-knew-how-many challenges to his leadership. And that would mean Audrey would be packless with me.

Of course, I wonder what people would say if Bishop left the pack as well. Would they change their minds?

"Just point me in the right direction," Deacon said, his wolf rising to the surface and his enormous alpha power slipping out of his control for a second. "They'd never question my judgment when it comes to protecting the pack. And she *is* pack."

He stood, a wildness in his eyes I'd never seen before. He was always joking, always laughing, but when it came to Audrey, he was dead serious. My shy, gentle mate had won over a man who kept everyone at arm's length with a well-placed quip.

"The cart at the north gate is waiting for us. Cyrus sent our packs and supplies ahead so we just need to get there." His gaze dipped to Audrey. "Do you want to wake her, carry her, or have me carry her?"

AUDREY

Knox woke me with a soft mental nudge and a kiss to my forehead. His wood smoke scent filled my senses first, warm and comforting, then I opened my eyes and fell into wolf-darkened orbs flecked with brilliant shards of green.

Mine. My mate.

Then everything came crashing back. The attack, Bishop being poisoned, and the sea of emotions threatening to drown me. My throat tightened even as I tried to control my emotions for Knox's sake.

"It's time to go," he said his voice gruff. But I knew he wasn't upset with me. Beneath the drowning sea of desperation and fear was his love for me.

We could do this. We could save Bishop. We *would* save Bishop.

"Right." I sat up and moved out of the way and put my

boot back on as Deacon and Knox dressed Bishop in a shirt and pair of pants.

I wasn't sure when Deacon had arrived, but it made sense for someone to help Knox or in the very least someone to bring clothes since I doubted Knox could leave Bishop's side at the moment, even if he wanted to.

It also made sense that it wasn't Cyrus since he had to get someone ready to take over running the pack while he was away, for which I was grateful. I still had no idea how to react to Cyrus after he'd apologized, and I still wasn't one hundred percent sure it hadn't been a stress-induced — or Sterling-induced — hallucination.

"Ready?" Deacon asked as he handed Knox this realm's equivalent of a kilt, something the huntmaster only ever wore. I'd never seen him in anything else and even though we'd had dinner a few times while Knox was away hunting for the pack, it was still a struggle not to ogle him.

How could I not? The man was built, each muscle mouth-wateringly defined, and the kilt put almost all of it on display. He also radiated a sharp feral quality and was constantly releasing a trickle of alpha power, unable to fully contain the force within him that was just as strong as Bishop, Knox, and possibly even Cyrus.

All of that equaled a magnetic pull that made it hard to look away... well hard if he hadn't been standing beside Knox.

Knox was a pull on my soul that I couldn't deny and didn't want to. It didn't matter that he was gorgeous, his body just as beautifully defined as Deacon's, his face the picture of a dark angel. I'd have loved him regardless of his stunning looks because he was mine, but having a handsome mate certainly didn't hurt.

Knox wrapped the kilt around his waist then pulled Bishop into his arms, easily lifting him.

"You good?" Deacon asked, turning his attention to me, the deep laugh lines around his eyes crinkling and his lips quirking as if he'd thought of something amusing but wasn't going to share with the class. "Need me to carry you?"

Knox groaned and glared at him, making Deacon chuckle and me feel like I'd missed part of a conversation.

"You know I had to offer," Deacon said with a shrug.

"You know she'd have asked for help if she wanted it," Knox huffed.

"*You* know she wouldn't," Deacon shot back.

"And you both know I'm standing right here," I cut in before the conversation continued as if I weren't around. "I'm fine for now, thank you," I told Deacon. "And I'll ask for help if I need it. I learned the first time after not mentioning my blisters."

Deacon cocked an eyebrow, drawing my attention to his golden brown eyes that were bright with curiosity. "Blisters?"

"She walked north until her feet bled and didn't tell anyone. Not even Bishop," Knox replied as we hurried away from my semi-private patio toward the Residence's gate and the town beyond.

My foot throbbed with every step, and I gritted my teeth, trying to keep my gait as even as possible while acknowledging the irony of the conversation. Knox and Bishop needed me to be strong and I couldn't afford for Cyrus to think I was too weak to travel with them even if he'd said I was going and had apologized for his earlier behavior.

He could still change his mind and I'd fight him again if I had to, but I'd rather not. Looking like I was going to be useful and not a burden was the best place to start.

"I was trying to not be a nuisance," I said, somehow finding myself half walking half jogging between Bishop and Deacon because of their much longer legs.

"And not trying to prove you could keep up with experienced hunters," Deacon chuckled, ruffling my hair as if I were an annoying little sister. "Sure you were."

"Hands off," Knox growled.

A possessive anger rushed through our bond, and his wolf fully darkened his eyes, taking over.

"You bet." Deacon took a step away and raised his hands. "But you know you're not the one in charge. She is."

"And if she wants you to touch her, she'll tell you," Knox's wolf snarled with a sharp glare before turning away from the main road and taking a dark, narrow alley even though the light was still the pre-dawn gray before the sunrise and the streets were empty.

Despite the lack of people around, I could still feel

the tension building inside Knox, the one that screamed too close, too tight, not enough space and sky and air.

Of course, I had no idea if this was how he always felt walking through Stonehaven or if the current circumstances were exacerbating his claustrophobia. Which didn't really matter. He needed me to get through this just like I needed him.

I placed my hand against his arm and sent as much love as I could muster with my own emotions going crazy.

With a groan, he sucked in a deep breath, some of the tension melting away as I helped steady his soul, and we hurried forward, rushing down dark alley after dark alley, Deacon not saying a word about our route.

A moment later, we reached a main road leading up to a large square only fifty feet ahead where Cyrus, Whil, and Nova waited beside a cart big enough to fit Bishop and Knox and our supplies.

The cart was plain — no decoration or even a coat of paint — had four wheels so whoever was pulling didn't also have to hold up the front, and a push bar that had been wrapped in fabric to cushion the pusher's hands.

Someone had laid out a pile of blankets on the cart bed, and Knox laid Bishop on top of them. Just above Bishop's head were five travel packs, and two sturdier packs that were, without a doubt, waterproof and likely held Whil's books and supplies.

"Up you go, Audrey," Cyrus said his voice strange, still gruff but also strained as if he didn't know how to speak to me anymore.

He gestured to the cart without hesitation and a tension that had blended in with all the other things worrying me eased. I wasn't going to have to fight my instincts and work up the nerve to argue with him again.

"Stay off your foot for two days. Give it time to heal," Nova said as Whil climbed into the cart with me, and Knox stepped to the side and held Bishop's hand.

"The pack is yours and Lucius's," Cyrus said to Nova. He ducked under the cart's push bar and got into position while Deacon tossed his kilt into the cart and shifted into his large gray wolf. "Keep an ear on the rumor mill."

Nova gave him a knowing look and nodded her understanding.

If I hadn't been so worried about saving Bishop and keeping Knox sane, Cyrus's comment would have renewed my uncertainty about being accepted by the pack. Sure there'd been nice people at the festival, but there'd still been those who'd felt brave enough to give me dirty looks even while I was with Bishop. Which meant there were others who'd smiled at me because of Bishop but still didn't like me.

Which wasn't a problem to worry about. Not until we'd saved Bishop.

Nothing else would matter if he died.

AUDREY

WE TRAVELED ALL DAY, NOT STOPPING FOR LUNCH BECAUSE Whil and I were the only ones who needed it and we ate in the cart. Bishop's convulsions started increasing in severity and frequency by mid-morning, and I helped Whil pour another elixir into his mouth and held him steady until I was sure he'd swallowed it.

Tension filled the air and Knox's worry churned with heavy dread inside me. It also didn't help that the road, while wide enough for two carts to pass side by side, was boxed in with rock walls that grew taller and taller the farther we went, adding his claustrophobia to his fear of losing his brother.

No one said anything until just before sunset when we reached a tall, wide but shallow cavern in the rock big enough for half a dozen carts to mostly stay under the shelter of the rock overhang and four or five more beyond it. At the back, protected from the elements on three sides sat a squat stone building with a metal door and two windows framed by metal shutters.

"This is our stop for the night," Cyrus said, pushing the cart halfway to the building and securing the front two wheels with a nifty locking system that involved the lock on the wheel and a wire running up to a locking handle built into the push bar.

Behind me, Deacon shifted back into his human form and shut a large metal gate, securing the enormous alcove from outside threats while Whil grabbed one of her waterproof packs and hopped off the back of the cart.

"This is a major road," she said, answering my unspoken question about why there was a house and a protected shelter beside the road when there wasn't anything or anyone else around. "There are three shelters along it before it comes out of the mountains."

I nodded my understanding and turned my attention back to the house. It was guaranteed shelter and it had a chimney, which meant not sleeping outside in the slightly cool summer night. And while it was easily twice as big as the patrol shed between Stonehaven and Anakar, nothing would be big enough for Knox the stay the entire night.

"Knox, Bishop, and I aren't staying in there," I said. It would tear Knox up having to fight his claustrophobia and his need to stay with his twin at the same time, and I wasn't going to allow that.

"Of course not," Cyrus said, pointing ten feet away to a scorched hole in the ground edged by fist-sized rocks.

"We'll make camp here. Whil and Deacon can stay inside if they want."

"Nah," Deacon said at the same time Whil replied, "I'm staying with Bishop in case anything changes."

"Do you think something will?" I asked, suddenly not wanting to leave Bishop's side, not even to just hop off the cart despite knowing I needed to move so Knox could carry him closer to the fire pit to keep him from getting cold during the night.

Pushing past that urge, I shifted to the edge of the cart to hop off.

"Stop!" Cyrus barked with a snap of power.

My pulse lurched and my muscles twitched, his power freezing me in place and sending a blast of instinctual fear racing through my body.

I squeezed my eyes shut, fighting my reaction before Knox lost it.

Cyrus apologized... maybe. He's not going to hurt me. He's not Sterling.

But damn, none of that, no matter how logical, could break a lifetime of conditioning, and I couldn't completely get rid of my concern.

"Nova said to stay off your feet for two days," he said as he hurried to my side. His voice was almost as gruff as Knox's, and his power softly stuttered as if he were trying to hold it in but couldn't, not completely, giving me a sense that he wasn't angry with me.

Without warning, he picked me up, and our eyes

locked, my plain brown to his deep, dark mossy green, and my breath caught in my throat.

The fantasy of him holding me as if I were precious and slowly pushing into me rushed through me, heating my cheeks, and for a second, the fantasy felt like so much more than just a dream. It felt real, like a memory I couldn't quite grasp, slipping between my mental fingers as I desperately tried to cling to it while that thing in my soul that said I could trust Cyrus, had *always* said I could trust him, fluttered, a barely-there warmth around my heart.

His eyes widened as if he felt it, too, and something pulled between us, some strange magnetic force that made me want to bury myself in his arms and wrap myself in his warm earthy scent.

It had to be the stress of the situation. My soul needed steadying, and I couldn't get that from Bishop or even Knox since my mates needed steadying more than I did. I was still wary of Cyrus... wasn't I? One apology that I wasn't even sure had happened didn't make up for terrifying me and then leaving me afraid of him for days. The only reason I'd connected with him in any way was because I was desperate for a stable, emotional foundation.

Which only made a part of me mourn the Cyrus I'd lost, the one who, when we were almost at the death god's temple, had encouraged me to think about my future. Even the one who, after the spell to break my bond with

Knox failed, had tried to convince me that being mated to Knox wasn't the end of my world.

I wanted that Cyrus back.

Was that the real Cyrus or was the alpha who'd yelled at me in the arena been the real one?

His gaze dipped to my lips, turning my embarrassment at thinking about having sex with him into desire.

No! Bad, Audrey. I wasn't supposed to want that from Cyrus. He'd made it perfectly clear he didn't want me, and I was supposed to be happy with my strange fantasy despite that small, barely audible voice inside my head that said he was mine, too.

Stress. It was stress, God damn it.

I didn't trust him.

But it was just so hard to remember that, not with his strong arms around me and him looking at me with a confusing mix of emotions that I couldn't quite recognize but was certain none were anger or disgust.

Then he jerked his attention away, shattering the moment and leaving me strangely breathless while wondering if we'd really shared a moment or if it had all been in my head again.

He carried me to the fire pit, set me on the ground, and straightened, his stern in-control alpha mask firmly back in place.

"Deacon," he growled before clearing his throat and making his voice sound more human. "Get enough wood from the shelter so Audrey can start a fire then go out and collect more in the forest. I'll get us something to eat."

Deacon raised an eyebrow at Cyrus, his lips quirking, but I couldn't figure out what was so funny.

"I need the run," Cyrus added before turning his back to me, pulling off his shirt, and stepping out of his pants, giving me a spectacular view of his powerful muscles and his amazing ass before he melted into his massive black wolf.

Whil opened the metal gate for him and he ran out, while Deacon pulled a pack from the cart, handed it to me, and went into the house.

A minute later, Whil had the blankets from the cart on the ground for Bishop, a pile of a few more blankets for the rest of us, and Deacon had returned from the house with an armful of wood, all while I sat there and watched, feeling selfish for not helping.

Except Cyrus hadn't let me get off the cart by myself and I was sure neither Whil nor Deacon would let me get up and walk around.

And really, just thinking about moving made me exhausted. It didn't matter that I'd sat in the cart all day. I'd barely gotten any sleep last night, an hour if I was lucky, and trying to keep it together to help Knox keep it together was beyond tiring.

Inside I was a screaming crying mess, clinging to myself with my mental fingernails while Knox's emotions threatened to drown me, adding to my own fear and heartache and grief.

All I wanted was to hold Bishop tight and never let go.

He was mine. He'd told me that he loved me and I hadn't gotten a chance to tell him back.

I wanted that chance. I wanted to stop being so selfish by demanding that he court me and just mate with him. We belonged together and there was a chance he wouldn't make it to the pool or that Whil's spell at the pool wouldn't work.

My throat tightened and tears burned my eyes, but I gritted my teeth and swallowed down my grief.

I had to stay strong and in control. Knox was counting on me. Through our bond, I could feel his grip on his human self weakening, and I could feel a fury that went beyond the most primal aspect of his wolf threatening to take over.

That was his true feral nature. It wasn't just his wolf, it went deeper, rooted in fear and a need to protect his human soul, whatever the cost, even if that meant burying his human half inside his wolf forever.

I didn't want Bishop to wake up to that, didn't want him to find his brother fully feral without anyone able to get him back.

I sent more love and confidence to Knox, knowing he could still feel all my worries but hoping that by showing him that I was being brave, he and his wolf could control his fear. Then I made a fire in the fire pit and used the starter in my pack to start it.

Deacon left through the gate and shut it behind him. The latch that could be opened from either side — if you had an opposable thumb — clicked into place and for a second there was nerve-racking silence only disturbed by the crackling fire.

"So," Whil said as she grabbed the second sturdy waterproof pack from the cart and sat beside me. "How are you doing?"

"I'm exhausted and sore."

Knox huffed, worry for me and not just Bishop swirling into the mix of emotions coming through the bond.

"Stay awake for dinner. You'll need your strength," he growled.

"I know," I told him.

I had no doubt that if I dozed off, Cyrus would use his power to wake me and make me eat, something I'd rather do on my own. But that thought didn't stop me from glancing at the blankets around Knox and Bishop and longing to just crawl under one and cling to my mates.

But food first!

I slapped my cheeks, forcing myself to stay awake and praying Cyrus caught something fast and it didn't take long to cook.

"From what you told me of your bond, it makes sense that you'd be exhausted," Whil said. "And I suspect it's not going to get much better."

"Swell."

"You should get Deacon or Cyrus to help you once we leave the road. I doubt you'll be able to keep Cyrus's pace all day." Whil huffed a soft laugh. "I'm not sure I'll be able to, either, but time is of the essence here."

As if to prove her point, Bishop groaned and his body went stiff, making my chest tighten. It wasn't a full blown convulsion, but it was the sign that the elixir was starting to wear off again.

Whil had explained the last time we'd given him an elixir that it was only a stopgap. All of its power was going toward slowing the poison, which meant it couldn't cure him — no amount of elixir would be able to remove it from his system — so there was no point in wasting an elixir by giving him more than one or two at a time. Even that wasn't enough to completely slow the poison down, which meant we were going to have to be giving him more elixirs closer and closer together so he could make it to the pool.

"Knox, help hold him," Whil said as she opened one of the packs, revealing that it was packed with elixir ampuls and lots of padding to ensure nothing broke.

Once Whil had given Bishop the elixir, we returned to an uncomfortable silence. It felt like everyone's worries were pressing down on me which made me acutely aware of my worry that Whil's block on the magical tether connecting me to Sterling had weakened. The last thing we needed right now was for me to go crazy.

"Whil." I shivered with a sudden chill and added another log to the fire. "After dinner, would you be able to check your block?" Because if she checked it now, I was guaranteed to pass out just like the other times she'd checked.

Knox stiffened at that. "You think that asshole might be influencing you?"

I squeezed his hand in reassurance. "I think I'm under a lot of stress and want to make sure the situation can't get worse."

"I checked it a few days ago and it was fine," Whil said. "But you're right. Better safe than sorry."

A few minutes later, Deacon returned with more firewood and Cyrus returned with a skinned and gutted animal the size of a large raccoon and a plucked and gutted bird the size of a chicken.

Just like when we'd been traveling north, I pretended our dinner hadn't been alive when Cyrus had caught it even though I knew it was silly and that I should have been used to it by now what with all the camping I'd already done.

On top of that, I was supposed to be a predator and I'd probably have no problems with killing an animal in wolf form. But unless a miracle happened, I'd never be a wolf, and I doubted I'd get over the idea of killing something.

Cyrus put the bird on the same collapsible spit we'd used the last time and Deacon set the firewood nearby then dropped his kilt — giving me an eyeful and making me hope the fire wasn't bright enough for everyone to see me blush. Then he shifted into his wolf and settled between Whil and Cyrus, resting his head in his paws and making me wonder if he was going to spend the night like that.

Which was a ridiculous thought. Why wouldn't he? His wolf was more comfortable in the elements, and he wouldn't need a blanket to keep the evening chill away... if there was much of a chill tonight. It was, after all, still summer and the temperature was still more or less comfortable.

Somehow, I managed to stay awake long enough to eat some dinner, then I snuggled in between Bishop and Knox and let Whil check the magical block in my head.

I knew I was supposed to close my eyes and just relax, but I couldn't stop looking at Bishop while she worked. He was so pale, his skin nearly white against the black and red veins covering his body. Sweat slicked his brow and his breathing was quick and shallow, which I supposed was better than convulsing and not breathing at all, but not by much.

The memory of dancing with him, of the joy and freedom, of having him whirl me around and around until I was breathless, clawed up to the front of my mind. Again, my throat tightened and tears burned my eyes. I tried, but this time I couldn't stop them from slowly leaking from my eyes.

He'd been so happy. The look in his eyes when he'd told me he loved me had stolen my breath, and he'd looked at me like I was amazing and beautiful, like I was the only woman in the world.

AUDREY

MY EYES CLOSED FOR A SECOND, OR AT LEAST I THOUGHT IT was a second. But when I opened them, I was no longer snuggled between Knox and Bishop, I was in the middle of the Residence's sacred grove.

Groggy, I sat up.

How had I—?

Right.

A dream.

I just hadn't had a dream like this since before Knox and I had sealed our bond.

Of course, it wasn't quite the same. The grove was only a few trees deep and beyond was a shimmering white wall. I glanced around. The wall was everywhere, even above me, which meant I was in a dome. The dream world, unlike all my previous dreams, was only as big as the shimmering bubble.

That, however, was the only thing that had changed

from my sexy dreams with Knox, and once again I wore my white transformation dress with my hair flowing loose around my shoulders and down my back.

Out of the corner of my eye, it looked blonder than it really was, with hints of shimmering gold when it was really just a drab dirty blond, and my skin was also brighter, as if I were summer fae and had a perpetual soft glow like Whil.

Rustling in the trees around me caught my attention, and I jerked my gaze away from my glowing skin, my heart racing. Having sexy times with Knox hadn't been the only thing that had happened in my dreams. Sterling had also invaded them, laughing at me, hurting me, convincing me I was worthless and an unwanted whore.

But instead of Sterling or Royce, Knox stepped into the grove—

No, not Knox. Bishop.

His expression was softer than Knox's and he didn't radiate that same amount of feral energy as his brother, so it had to be Bishop. And he looked healthy, no sign of the horrible discolored veins, his complexion warm and vibrant.

"Bishop!" I jumped to my feet and threw myself at him.

With a laugh, he caught me and spun me around, just like he had at the festival. And then just like the festival, he caught my lips in a searing kiss, making me feel his overwhelming love for me as if we were bonded like I was bonded with his brother.

It was so dazzling and wonderful, and so clearly a dream, that tears leaked from my eyes.

"Hey, beautiful," he murmured, pressing his forehead against mine and wiping my cheeks with his thumbs. "None of that."

"But you're dying, and I didn't get a chance to tell you that I love you." And I needed to. My heart would break if I didn't.

I leaned back so I could look into his warm brown eyes with their mesmerizing green flecks. He brushed a lock of hair away from my face, his expression gentle as if he knew how much I was hurting.

"I love you so much," I said.

I just wished I could tell him in person... not that I wasn't going to be able to tell him when Whil healed him because he'd survive this. He would. I just had to stay strong for a few days and then I could tell him and show him and do what I should have done with him from the beginning. Mate with him.

He'd shown me time and time again that he wanted to be my mate, but deep within me, I hadn't completely believed him, hadn't thought I could be worthy of the love from such an amazing, kind, generous man.

Maybe this Cinderella did have a prince... or rather two princes. They were night and day in their personalities but they were without a doubt mine.

"The moment you're awake, I'm telling you," I told dream-Bishop.

"You're telling me now." He cupped my cheek with his

large hand and I leaned into his touch, savoring the heat from his body and the warmth that radiated around my heart from our shifter connection.

It had only been a day, and I already missed this physical connection with its sense of affection and certainty and protection.

"I'm just telling a dream." My throat tightened, despite my determination to stay strong. "You're a figment of my imagination and I haven't told you anything yet."

"Audrey," he said, my name on his lips teasing desire down my body from my head to my quickly heating core. "I don't think this is a dream."

"I'm pretty sure I'm dreaming." And now I was arguing with my subconscious.

"No, I mean, it *is* a dream, but not in the way you think." He squeezed my hand and a red low-back couch with thick plush cushions appeared beside him. "This is *my* dream."

"How can it be your dream?"

He pointed to the shimmering dome above us. "My consciousness retreated into my mind and created a bubble in my dream world to keep out the pain of the poison. If we were in your dream world, the bubble wouldn't be there. You're sharing my dream."

"I just want you back. That's why I'm dreaming this." It was the only explanation that made sense.

"You know that's not true." He sat, pulled me into his lap, and wrapped me in a warm, protective embrace. "Knox and I often share dreams, usually when he's hunting and beyond the reach of our twin bond. With you mate bonded with him, it doesn't surprise me that you're able to join us."

But then that would mean the wild sex with Knox that I'd dreamed about when I'd first arrived in this realm hadn't just been my fantasy.

It had been Knox's as well.

Oh, no.

He'd known about us having wild dream sex. Hell, he'd started all of it as if he hadn't been able to control himself and he hadn't said a thing to me.

A branch cracked behind me, drawing my attention as Knox stormed into the grove. His eyes were dark and he radiated the same kind of barely contained energy he'd had in our previous dreams.

"Took you long enough," Bishop said, patting the seat beside him.

"We're on guard," he growled. "I don't want to be here." His gaze slid to mine, his expression turning hungry. "Mate."

With a snarl, he was on me, tangling his fingers in my hair and kissing me like I was his only source of oxygen. Heat erupted in my body, pooling between my thighs, and I was aching and ready in an instant.

My soul cried out for him, for his strength and our connection, and I grabbed the front of his pants and yanked on the tie holding them up, not caring that I was in Bishop's arms or that this was the real Knox in my dream—

Crap.

"You didn't tell me we were having shared dreams," I gasped trying to shove him away and failing.

"Would you have fucked him if you knew?" Knox—no, his wolf asked. "You. Are. Mine." He yanked on my hair, sending more pleasure rushing through me. "I wasn't giving you up because he was afraid. And I'm not stopping because you know the truth."

He dipped in and nipped my neck. Another bolt of pure lust soaked into my dress and I squirmed in Bishop's lap.

I wanted him. I wanted *both* of them, and my body didn't care I was supposed to be upset with Knox for lying through omission.

"Fuck, Audrey," Bishop hissed as he shifted his hips, his hard length digging into my thigh. "You like him like this?"

I opened my mouth to deny it but couldn't. Even if this was a dream, I was sure both of them could smell how turned on I was.

"Answer him," Knox barked, a burst of his power snapping into me and making my own dream power rise up and snap back. "Do you like when I take over his human body and fuck you senseless?"

I nodded, my voice gone and my mouth dry in anticipation.

"Tell him." Knox's wolf tightened his grip in my hair and shoved a hand inside the front of my dress. "Tell him."

"I do," I gasped.

He squeezed my breast adding another point of pressure verging on pain and my breath picked up with need.

"Tell him."

"I love it," I moaned. Because I did. I loved the wildness, the fierceness, and the passion.

When Knox's wolf fucked me in our dreams, I felt overwhelmed in the best way and yet also powerful. Powerful because I made this ferocious man wild with lust, and powerful because he brought out a ferociousness in me that I'd never had in real life.

Not before I'd yelled at Cyrus last night... hunh?

"And you're going to love it when *both* of your mates fuck you," Knox said, jerking my attention back to him.

Did I want to have sex with both of them?

My body quivered in anticipation.

Hell, yes I did.

AUDREY

I WANTED THEM BOTH IN THIS DREAM *AND* WHEN I WAS awake. I wanted it all with them. Forever.

Mine, that small voice in my head growled.

Yes. They. Were.

I tore open the front of Knox's pants, something I could only do because this was a dream. His hard cock, thick and long, jutted proudly from his body and my mouth watered at the memory of taking him in my mouth in Whil's greenhouse library.

Somehow he'd known exactly what I'd wanted *and* what I'd needed to get past my insecurities. Of course, he'd already experienced me without any inhibitions in our shared dreams. He knew what I looked like when I ached for him and knew I loved it when he overwhelmed me.

I teased my fingers over his tip, dragging them

through the precum gathering at his slit, then pumped my hand down his length.

He groaned, the sound long and low and growly, going straight to my core.

"Damn that's hot, beautiful," Bishop purred, his warm breath washing over my cheek and neck, teasing already hypersensitive nerves. "Can you make him come with just that?"

Knox huffed. "Maybe my human but not me. I'm saving it for when I'm buried in her hot pussy. But you—" He narrowed his eyes, capturing me in their bottomless dark depths. "You're denying your other mate. He wants to eat you out."

"He does, does he?" Bishop asked with a chuckle, even as his pupils dilated with desire.

Knox's wolf sneered back at him. "Don't you? All that dripping nectar going to waste? Unless you want to bury yourself in her. She doesn't need a warm up in our dreams." His sneer deepened and he tore my dress from my body. "And she'll come all night."

Bishop's gaze jumped to my breasts then sank lower to my curls and he drew in a deep breath. "I want to bury my face between your thighs, breathe in your scent, and make you come on my tongue."

His words sent the tremor of an orgasm racing through me. "Yes." *Please yes. God yes!*

The couch turned into a bed and Bishop fell back so he was lying down.

Knox, with his grip still in my hair, turned my head,

forcing me to look at him. "Straddle his face." Then he gripped my hand around his cock, squeezing tight but not making it move. "And don't you dare stop."

I shifted so I straddled Bishop, and he grabbed my hips with his large hands and dragged me up his body. With a groan, he shoved his nose in my curls and breathed in my scent then released his breath, teasing my sensitive folds.

I shuddered at the sensation, my breath already ragged with anticipation.

"Audrey," Knox growled with a tug on my hair, and I realized I wasn't moving my hand.

Damn. This multiple partners thing was harder than I anticipated and we'd barely begun.

Somehow, I managed to heave my attention away from Bishop still just teasing me with his breath, and slowly dragged my hand up to Knox's tip, dampen it with more precum then pumped back down. Hard.

"That's it," he purred, his voice rumbling low in his chest. "Don't stop."

"Yes—"

Bishop teased his tongue through my folds and I forgot what I was going to say.

Sensation flooded me, his tongue teasing and licking and dipping inside me. My thighs burned with the effort to hold myself up and not suffocate him, and Knox's hard length somehow grew harder and bigger with each stroke of my hand.

I tried to keep my hand moving, but couldn't maintain my concentration, not with the tingling heat building in my core.

"Mate." Knox's wolf tugged on my hair and a shiver, not quite an orgasm, but heading in that direction, teased and tormented me.

I heaved my attention to him, but Bishop flicked his tongue against my clit and my thoughts scattered.

Oh, fuck.

My eyes rolled back as I reached the precipice. But instead of taking me over the edge, Bishop drew back and the feeling slipped away, making me whine in disappointment.

"Mate," Knox growled.

I dragged myself back to him and he captured my jaw, forcing me to look at him.

"You keep stopping," he snarled. "Open up."

My pulse lurched then leaped into a wild tattoo and I eagerly opened. The bed magically shrank, getting lower into the perfect position, and Knox smeared his precum over my lips with a teasing slide of his tip.

Before I could lick it away, he yanked on my hair, angling my head back as far as it would go, and held my chin in place, forcing me open.

With a snarl, he plunged inside with a thrust more powerful than any he'd made the other night. His cock hit the back of my throat then went deeper, blocking my breath for a nerve-racking, thrilling second before he jerked out.

Wild desire burned in his eyes and his canines extended.

"Audrey?" Bishop asked, brushing a finger across my cheek. "Are you okay with this?"

I nodded and Knox slapped his cock against my lips.

"Use words," he commanded. "Do you want me to fuck your mouth in a way that can only happen here? Do you want us to make you see stars?"

"Yes," I moaned, and Knox plunged back into my mouth while Bishop continued to tease me with his tongue, bringing me to the edge again and again but not letting me fall over.

I gasped and moaned, unable to concentrate on anything except the desire building inside me, grateful that all I had to do was let go and let the guys bring me pleasure.

A small part of me, the part that was raised in the mortal realm that was shy about sex and nudity, wondered if I should be feeling used, especially by Knox who was fucking my throat with a wild fury that made it nearly impossible to catch my breath and had tears spilling from my eyes and drool leaking from my mouth.

But it felt too good. I could feel Knox's wild passion even though the emotions from our bond were muted in this dream world. I could also feel his power rising, teasing and taunting mine into a ferocious dance of longing and lust.

I did that. *I* made him wild and hungry.

He wanted me so much, desired me so deeply, that he couldn't hold himself back.

Then Bishop flicked his tongue on my clit, heaving my attention back to him. He wasn't as wild, the human half of his soul still in control, but I could feel an intensity radiating from him, more powerful than any I'd felt before.

He wanted me just as much as Knox did. But where Knox lost control, Bishop took it, possessing my body, refusing to let me come until he decided I could.

"Mate," Knox snarled, his eyes completely black, his power crackling over my skin. "Fuck."

He jerked out of my mouth and Bishop shoved two fingers inside me and sucked on my clit.

Fireworks exploded inside me, stealing my breath and sending bone-melting bliss racing into every cell in my body. The world went bright white, and I spun around and around and then found myself face down on the bed.

A slightly out-of-focus Bishop aimed a wolfish grin at me as strong hands seized my hips and jerked me up to my knees.

"Scream for me, Audrey," Knox growled, plunging his hard-as-steel thick cock inside me with a powerful stroke.

He bottomed out, the impact driving me into the bed, knocking the air from my lungs, and sending the tremor of another climax tingling up my spine.

"Who's your mate?"

My eyes rolled back with pleasure. I didn't know why

it turned me on so much when Knox fucked me like a maniac and demanded I name him my mate.

In real life, I didn't want to submit to him or anyone even though my instincts kept me doing it. I'd spent too much time living in fear and cowering, but in this dream world — and while I was awake, if I was being honest with myself — I wanted to submit to Knox during sex. I wanted all his ferocious power and desire claiming me as his, wanted his strength and wild power protecting me. Wanted to always be his.

"Who." He slammed into me again. "Is." Another thrust that had me seeing stars and my core tightening in anticipation. "Your. Mate?"

"You," I gasped, power roaring up inside me, whirling around and through Knox's in a wild primal dance not of dominance or submission but of lust and competition between equals.

"Who?" His pace turned wild and he reached around and rubbed violent circles against my clit, lighting me up, driving my need higher and higher.

Oh, God.

The pleasure that had roared back to life the second he'd thrust into me tightened, lighting up every nerve in my body and the precipice was suddenly there. Right there.

Then, with another thrust, I careened over the edge.

"You," I screamed. "You are, Knox."

With a roar, he slammed home, wrapped his body around mine, and sank his teeth into my shoulder. His muscles jerked with the force of his release and he filled me with hot jets of cum and power and light and oh!

Stars snapped behind my lids and again I was whirling, glowing, floating on a consuming bliss that stole all sight and sound, leaving me with only amazing sensation.

AUDREY

THIS TIME, WHEN I CAME TO, I WAS STILL LYING FACE DOWN on the mattress and looking into Bishop's warm brown eyes. Knox was still buried inside me, his tongue laving the wound he'd made in my shoulder and his body still vibrating with power.

"Hi," Bishop said, and he brushed a lock of sweaty hair from my forehead. Lust still filled his eyes, but it was softened with a breathtaking love.

My heart swelled, the warmth I felt when I was with him building, filling me with certainty. Just like wild Knox with his even wilder wolf was mine, so, too, was gentle, generous Bishop.

"Kiss me," I told him.

Knox nuzzled my neck then pulled out and helped me roll over and lie on my back while keeping a hand on my stomach.

Bishop didn't seem to care that Knox was still

touching me. He settled himself over me, holding himself up on his elbows and dipping close until our foreheads touched, creating a private cocoon for just the two of us.

"As my mate commands," he said, his voice soft and reverent, and he slowly pressed his lips against mine.

Warmth billowed around my heart and seeped outward, sinking deep into every nerve, fiber, and cell in my body.

Home.

This was home. Everything about Bishop reassured me that I was finally safe, finally loved, finally home.

Knox was my freedom, my primal wildness that only appeared in my dreams, and Bishop was my shelter in the storm.

"You're so amazing, Audrey," Bishop murmured against my lips. "So beautiful and determined and brave. I knew the minute I saw you that you were special. I love you so much."

"I love you, too," I said, my eyes burning with tears. I'd waited my whole life for someone to say those words to me and I never wanted to let him go. I wanted to stay in this dream forever, making love to Bishop and Knox.

But that wouldn't help save him. If I didn't wake up, it would only make things more complicated and I *had* to save him.

"Hey," he said, nuzzling my cheek as if he could sense my shift of emotions. "It's okay. We can just cuddle for the rest of the dream."

"No." Never. I wanted him closer, *needed* him closer.

The compulsion surged within me, and I tangled my fingers in his hair and drew him down so I could kiss him again.

"I want you to make love to me," I told him. I wanted the awe and tenderness from our first time together.

"Always," he whispered, his expression filled with a soul-deep affection. "Forever."

He captured my lips in a passionate kiss and slowly pushed inside me, drawing out my aching yearning until finally — finally! — he was deep inside me.

Our shifter connection deepened and for a second, I felt as connected with him as I did with Knox when I was awake.

Then he started to move, a slow slide out and a just as slow push back in. Each stroke dragged against my hypersensitive channel, rebuilding the heat he'd ignited with his tongue before Knox had made me see stars and sinking it deep inside me, strengthening our connection.

In and out.

Slow and steady.

Driving me higher and higher, making me breathless with anticipation.

"Bishop," I moaned, my hips bucking into his thrust, desperate for more friction.

My core ached with a deep thrumming desire, my whole body tense with the buildup of his sensual strokes despite his agonizingly slow pace.

"So beautiful," Bishop said, sitting back and grabbing

my hips to hold me still, taking full control of my pleasure. "Let me make you feel good."

He withdrew to just the tip, and my inner muscles
fluttered with his withdrawal, needing him back inside
me, filling me. Then he thrust back in, a little harder than
before, sending desire shivering through me.

A moan escaped my lips and my eyes rolled back as I
gave in to him. I focused on where our bodies connected,
on the sensual thrusts igniting every nerve in my core
and the warmth around my heart.

The wildness I sometimes had in these dreams lazily
rose from deep within me and Bishop matched it. Our
dream-powers caressed and entwined in a slow primal
dance. It filled my senses with everything that was
Bishop, power and affection and comfort.

"Sisters, Audrey," Bishop groaned, his pace picking
up, his control starting to slip.

I dragged my eyes open and met his gaze, falling into
a bottomless brown warmth filled with green stars. I
could feel his desire on the edge of breaking free of his
hold as well as his love and pride and awe.

The feelings astounded me. People didn't feel things
like that for me. I was weak. I couldn't shift. I could only
dream that someone as powerful and handsome as
Bishop would want to be with me.

But it wasn't just a dream. He wanted me in real life. It
wasn't a trick and I wasn't imagining it.

He wanted me and he was *mine*.

The thought made my soul sing and my power

billowed stronger, igniting around my heart and rushing into every part of my body.

God, I loved this man. I loved him with the very depths of my soul.

He pumped harder and faster into me, and my desire spiraled higher.

"Yes, Bishop," I moaned. *Yes yes yes.*

His hips jerked, and his rhythm stuttered as he struggled to maintain his pace. The brown warmth of his gaze darkened as his wolf rose to the surface and the feelings rushing between us turned molten, everything else forgotten. All that remained was our overwhelming need.

An inferno roared around my heart and my muscles shook. I squirmed in his grip, unable to control myself, desperate to buck up to meet him, and couldn't catch my breath. Our dream-powers writhed, swirling faster and faster, building higher and higher, and I couldn't look away from him.

I was on fire, desperate for a release and yet desperate to hold on as long as possible even as the pressure threatened to burn me up.

And then he rubbed my clit and pleasure exploded through my body.

Oh, God.

He roared his own release and every muscle in my body contracted, locking us together and capturing me in a blazing inferno of bliss. The pleasure spun me around and around, green stars flashing across my vision, and a deep booming gong roared through me.

It dragged my essence into its consuming reverbera-
tions and brilliant golden light surrounded us. I fell
deeper and deeper into his eyes, his soul, his very
essence, spinning around and around, our powers— No,
our souls, merging into a blazing golden tapestry.

Mine.

The tapestry flared, locking into place and connecting
my soul to Bishop's.

Yes, yours. Always.

CYRUS

AUDREY WOKE WITH A SHARP GASP, JERKED UPRIGHT, AND pressed her hands over her heart, her eyes wide.

"Audrey." I scrambled to my feet to get to her on the other side of the campfire. I didn't know what had shocked her awake — probably a bad dream — all I knew was that I had to reassure her. Her other mates were still unconscious which meant it was up to me—

My thoughts stuttered at that.

Not *other* mates.

That would imply I was also her mate.

Her mates were still asleep. She only had two.

Whil sat up as well, though not nearly as quick to react as me. Still, she was closer. She'd been dozing close to the three of them since she and I had given Bishop his late-night dose of elixir. I should let her comfort Audrey or whatever the hell she needed.

But my wolf was determined and there was no way I was going to be able to fight the compulsion.

"Oh, my," Whil gasped as she squinted at Audrey with her head cocked to the side.

"Oh my, what?" I asked as I reached for Audrey. "Audrey, what?"

So far neither Audrey nor Whil looked upset, suggesting nothing horrible had happened to Bishop, but still— They were both stunned.

"Audrey," I pressed, capturing her chin with my fingers and forcing her to look at me, my pulse racing. Was she hurt and too stunned to register it or had something else happened? "What?"

"I..." Myriad emotions flashed across her expression: confusion, longing, shock before setting on nervous and she pulled away from my touch.

My wolf snarled at the loss of contact, especially because it looked like she was afraid of us, but I managed to stay where I was and crossed my arms so I wouldn't touch her again.

But then I realized that made me look angry at her.

I dropped my arms to my side but that didn't feel right, either.

Fuck. How was Bishop always so relaxed around her? If I was courting her, I'd be holding her tight and never letting her go, which of course, would only piss her off and damage her grown confidence and desire for independence.

Fuck fuck fuck.

"I suppose I shouldn't be surprised," Whil said.

"Surprised about what!" I barked, my power snapping out of my control and waking Knox and Deacon who both tensed, ready for danger.

I hated surprises. I couldn't protect her if there was something I didn't know. Everything within me screamed that I needed to fix whatever had happened. Now now now.

Whil flashed me a bittersweet smile. "She just mate bonded with Bishop."

"She—" I wrenched my attention back to Audrey, who was shrinking in on herself before Knox wrapped his arms around her and tugged her close. "You—"

How could she have mate bonded with him? He wasn't even conscious and I'd been on watch for the second half of the night. I would have noticed if Bishop had woken up.

Well, if I hadn't believed in fated mates before, I do now," Deacon said in my head, his wolf chuffing with wolfy laughter.

"That's impossible," I spat out, still stunned.

Shit. I hadn't meant to say that.

Just because we thought her mating bond with Knox formed because of her incomplete bond didn't mean that was what really happened.

In fact, she'd already proven that deep down, locked away — possibly for good — were strong alpha powers. She was an alpha, and that could mean with the curse she had all of the downsides and none of the advantages.

She could have mate bonded with Knox and Bishop because she needed to. At her power level, she'd need three mates at the minimum to get her through a heat without her developing a fever.

Except bonding with Bishop now was a disaster. She was in even more danger than before and there wasn't anything I could do about it.

"I didn't mean to," she said, her voice soft but her spine straightening. "But I don't regret it."

"Of course you meant it," Knox growled, glaring at me. "You and Bishop are meant to be mates."

"But if we can't save Bishop, you'll die," I snapped.

"I'll keep her safe," Knox snarled back.

"You'll be fucking insane!" More of my power stuttered out of control and Audrey winced but didn't shrink in on herself like before.

Fuck. I hadn't meant to say any of that, either.

Sisters, I needed to stop talking. I'd been certain their bond had already been forming when she'd stood her ground and somehow awakened her alpha power to defy me and stay by his side. I should have expected that she wouldn't need the formal declaration to awaken the magic in a shifter's soul that created mating bonds.

Why the hell was I freaking out about it?

But the thought of losing my brothers *and* Audrey made my heart race. Yes, I was determined to save Bishop, but I couldn't guarantee it. Not everything was in my control — no matter how hard I tried to control everything.

Hell, at the moment, it looked like any control I possessed was pure fantasy.

"It still needs to be sealed," Whil said to Audrey. "But we're only four or five days away from the pool. I'd suggest waiting until we're back in Stonehaven and have more privacy, but that's probably not reasonable with how your incomplete bond with Knox set off your heat."

Audrey's eyes widened and her breath picked up as panic tightened her expression. "You mean I could go into heat again even though it's only been about three weeks since my last one and I'm not supposed to have my next one for another five months?"

"A strong mating bond can set off an early heat," Whil said, not easing any of Audrey's fears.

My pulse lurched. I couldn't let her go into heat again in the middle of nowhere. Sure, she wouldn't put off dealing with it like the last time, but the chances of her having heat fever again with her alpha power level and only one conscious mate, me, and Deacon to help were too high — since non-bonded mates weren't as effective at keeping the heat fever at bay.

Everything that could go wrong with Audrey had, and she could still end up in the same dangerous situation she'd been in with her first heat because of her incomplete bond with Bishop.

And fuck me, the signs of her heat had started showing her first night in Stonehaven, two days after we'd found her. With her luck, it would hit just as fast and harder now.

Fear squeezed around my heart. If Bishop died, she wouldn't be able to seal her bond. Would she end up stuck in a heat fever until it killed her?

"Bishop and I will get you through it," Knox reassured her, nuzzling her neck in an attempt to get her to relax.

Except that was only if her heat didn't start until after we reached the pool and if Bishop survived.

But you can help, my wolf snarled at me. *Like you did last time.*

Still a terrible option, I huffed back. *We're not going to be able to walk away from her and that makes her a target. We can't be with her until the pack can see her for who she really is.*

And then?

The memory of being captured in her gaze when I'd lifted her out of the cast last night flashed through me. She'd been so soft and warm, and her sweet scent had enveloped me, seeping into my soul. The urge to kiss her had been overwhelming and it hadn't just come from my wolf. *I* wanted to wrap myself around her, plunge inside her, and bind my soul to hers.

She was mine. She'd always be mine.

I just needed to be patient and wait for my pack to fall in love with her, too. Then I'd be free to court her.

Except I was a disaster at courting women. I didn't know what to say and my responsibilities to the pack took up a lot of my time.

But even that thought couldn't snuff out the tiny

spark that had ignited in my soul at the idea that one day Audrey could be my mate.

I ached for her smile, her caress... her everything, and I'd been torturing myself by trying to make her hate me while keeping my distance from her.

It had taken everything within me to not look at her or stand close to her when I'd shown her to the community center for Nova's first aid class the other day, and my control had slipped when I'd had to ensure the room was safe for her.

I hadn't been happy that Danica and her followers were in the class but knew Zavier and Quinn would protect Audrey. Micah and Hazel wouldn't have been as aggressive in Audrey's defense as Zavier or even Quinn, but they, too, would have stood up for her.

I wasn't going to last until everyone in my pack had gotten their heads out of their asses. Except I had to, especially if it had been a member of my pack who'd tried to murder Audrey... a thought that made me furious and one I really didn't want to accept.

I couldn't believe that anyone in my pack was capable of murdering the mate of one of their alphas. They had to know Knox would go feral and we'd never get him back if Audrey died. Not to mention if Knox lost it, there was a chance Bishop would lose it, too.

Were there members who were so disgruntled with our leadership that they wanted to destroy us?

If so, they had to be serious in their hate, enough to get an extremely rare magic poison.

Was it one person? More?

I shoved those thoughts aside. So far there was no proof the man who'd attacked Audrey and Bishop had been a pack member, and there was nothing I could do about it right now. I had to get Bishop to the pool and save him then pretend to not know when he and Audrey sealed their bond and not be jealous about it. Which was another impossibility I doubted I'd be able to control.

When we got back, I'd ensure Audrey was safe, even if I had to be by her side all day every day... except that could only happen if she didn't go into heat and if Bishop survived and sealed their bond.

AUDREY

Cyrus's expression turned hard, and a wave of his power rolled over me, squeezing my chest and compelling me to submit. But I ground my teeth together and resisted everything within me screaming to make myself small and get as close to Knox as possible.

Cyrus had apologized for saying those horrible things to me and Whil had confirmed her magic was still keeping Sterling out of my head. Which meant my instinct that I could trust him came from within me.

And so did that damn fantasy that I couldn't get out of my head.

It had flared to life the moment Whil had mentioned the possibility of another heat, and I tried to shove it out of my mind, but it was stuck there, on replay. Cyrus holding me like I was precious as he pushed inside me. Kissing me like he cared for me.

Damn it. I shouldn't be thinking of Cyrus. I should be

thinking of my mate— *mates*. That shared dream had been so hot, my cheeks were flaming with embarrassment. Knox had taken me like he always had in our dreams, wild and ferocious, claiming my body like no one else could. And then Bishop—

God, Bishop. He was so sweet and sensual. Sex with him had been the complete opposite of Knox but just as sexy. It made my heart swell with love, and I felt our new impossible bond pulsing with warmth and spikes of pain.

Somehow, the connection we'd made in our dream, the overwhelming sense of belonging and claiming, was real.

But that wasn't possible. It had just been a hot as hell dream. Even if we'd said the vows to each other, a bond shouldn't have formed because we'd been asleep.

Of course, my bond with Knox shouldn't have been possible, either.

And yet I'd known the moment Bishop had been hurt that I couldn't live without him, that something inside me would shatter and I wouldn't be able to recover.

Had that compulsion been our bond? Had it already started to form before we'd been attacked? And how the hell had I done it without saying the words or even being conscious?

And it had to be me. I was the only common denominator between bonding with Knox and bonding with Bishop.

Did that mean my soul would randomly bond with anyone?

Cyrus sat back on his heels and pulled back his power. His expression was still hard, his gaze unfocused as if he were thinking about something serious. But despite that, my memories of the dream jumped back to my fantasy of him.

A shiver swept down my spine. Would whatever was broken inside me bond with anyone I was attracted to?

I couldn't let that happen. I couldn't accidentally mate bond with Cyrus. He'd despise me for the rest of our lives, and it wouldn't matter if the bond was supposed to make him fall in love with me or not.

He'd made it perfectly clear he didn't want me, and even if he'd apologized, that didn't mean he was suddenly in love with me... or that he even wanted to be my friend.

Congratulations, Deacon said in my head from where he sat on the other side of the campfire, still in his wolf form. *Bishop will be ecstatic with how your bond formed. Now no one can deny that you're meant to be together.*

"Oh, I'm sure someone will complain," Cyrus replied, indicating that Deacon had spoken to everyone and not just me.

The muscle in Cyrus's jaw flexed and he ran his hands through his mussed hair. The braid running from the top of his head to the nape of his neck had almost completely fallen apart and most of his hair hung loose in silky brown waves that would make any girl jealous.

"I have no doubt someone will accuse her of having unnatural magic and that she imprisoned Bishop in a bond against his will," he added.

"Of course they would," I groaned. People were assholes and I'd just taken the pack's most eligible bachelor off the market.

Which only firmed my determination that there was no way in hell I was going to risk accidentally bonding with Cyrus.

Knox's emotions churned stronger through the bond, his anger rising to the surface as he battled to stay in control of himself and not let the feral nature of his wolf take over.

"I won't let them hurt you," he— no, his wolf snarled. "I'll challenge anyone who says you and Bishop aren't fated for each other. They might have forgotten that I'm their alpha, but I am. They won't disrespect what's mine."

"And I won't stop you," Cyrus replied, a strange look flashing in his eyes before disappearing behind his usual hard mask. "But before we do that, we need to make sure Bishop lives." He glanced at the sky that was now just starting to lighten with dawn. "Let's have breakfast and head out. I want to get to the next shelter early so we're well rested for the days after. The remaining days won't be easy."

With that, he grabbed the water bucket and headed to the house while Deacon shifted into his human form and gave me an eyeful before putting on his kilt and following him.

Whil grabbed our travel pot, which sat close to the fire with last night's leftovers, and got to work preparing breakfast.

I glanced around, looking for something to do so I wouldn't be useless even though my soul screamed to stay with Bishop and Knox and steady our souls.

Knox tightened his grip and buried his nose in my neck, drawing in my scent, and a violent flash of panic crashed through our bond, threatening to drag me under. He must have noticed my uncertainty about staying where I was or proving myself to Cyrus and the thought had shattered his control.

"I need you with me," he rumbled, his grip crushing me against his chest.

"It's okay," I gasped, trying to focus on pushing love and certainty to him, but a spike of Bishop's pain shot through our bond and I lost my concentration.

Knox growled, the sound low and dangerous, making Whil's eyes widen.

"I'm not going anywhere."

Concentrate. Push it out. Block it off. Something.

Incomplete thoughts whirled through me. Knox's fear and determination and love had had me clinging to myself and holding myself together when Bishop had been hurt, but add in Bishop's pain and it was too much.

"Knox," Whil said and my mate's gaze snapped to her. "She's got two bonds now. She's feeling what you're feeling from Bishop *and* all your emotions."

"Fuck," he snarled, and the whirlpool drowning me pulled back just enough to let me catch my breath. "I'm sorry, Audrey. I'm sorry." He relaxed his grip around me and nuzzled my neck in an attempt to soothe me. "It's just so hard. My wolf is freaking out. *I'm* freaking out."

"I know," I murmured back. "It'll be okay. We just need to hang on for a few more days and Bishop will be safe."

AUDREY

We ate breakfast, cleaned up our campsite for the next travelers, and repacked our travel packs. Once again, Cyrus wouldn't let me walk — even to go to the bathroom in the house at the back of the shelter, and I had to sneak a moment when his back was turned to stand on my bruised foot to see how it was doing.

It was still achy, but not nearly as bad as yesterday morning. Although I had no doubt it wouldn't be happy hiking for three or four days. Perhaps it would feel better tomorrow morning after another full day of being off it.

Cyrus opened the heavy gate protecting the shelter from monsters, and we got into our traveling positions with me, Whil, and Bishop in the cart, and Knox walking beside us, holding Bishop's hand. Much to my surprise, Cyrus took the job of scouting ahead and looking for trouble in his wolf form, leaving Deacon to push the cart.

I'd have thought Cyrus would have wanted to leave

the scouting to his huntmaster and stay with his brothers like he had for most of yesterday, but I wasn't going to complain. He probably had a lot on his mind, and I was still concerned about how upset he'd gotten when he learned I'd unconsciously formed another mating bond with one of his brothers.

If he wasn't near me, he couldn't yell at me and add to the stress I was already drowning under, and I couldn't accidentally mate bond with him.

Of course, he wasn't going to stay away forever, and I was going to have to figure out what to do about that.

I turned my attention to Bishop and swept a lock of hair away from his sweaty forehead, refocusing my thoughts on him. His complexion was ghostly and tinged with gray, not a good sign, and the ugly black and red veins covering his body had thickened while we'd been asleep.

My heart thudded hard, the weight of everything crushing inside my chest.

I *was* going to save him. I'd walk until my feet bled to get to the pool as quickly as possible because he was mine. My mate. He'd always been mine and always would be and I knew, even if he was unconscious, that he wanted to be my mate. He'd told me before we bonded that he loved me and again during our sexy shared dream.

The thought made my heart sing. I wasn't worried about figuring out our relationship — although we were still going to have to figure a few things out. There wasn't any resistance with Bishop. Not like there'd been with Knox. The biggest complication was going to be balancing my time between him and Knox, since there were situations where Knox wouldn't be able to be with us.

Of course, that only mattered if we got Bishop to the pool in time and Whil could magically pull the poison out of him.

"He's strong," Whil said as if she could read my thoughts when she was probably just seeing all my fears written on my face. "He'll make it."

"He will," I replied. He had to.

But the nagging voice of fear inside me, the one made stronger with the flood of Knox's emotions, worried that he wouldn't make it.

He'd said the shimmer surrounding the dream-grove had been his subconscious holding back the pain, but I'd seen thick black cracks in it just before I'd woken up. That mental protection was going to shatter and then he'd be in agony, even while he was unconscious.

Although maybe that had just been my imagination. I'd just had the most amazing dream sex and felt so connected with him that I'd somehow created a real mating bond between us.

Maybe seeing those cracks was my dream mind showing me a glimpse of my deepest fear because I was unable to truly trust my happiness. People didn't treat me the way Bishop did. I was weak and pathetic and—

No.

I lay down and snuggled against Bishop, suddenly needing all the physical contact I could get to strengthen our shifter connection and to push out those horrible thoughts that had been with me all my life.

The thoughts weren't true. Bishop wasn't the only one who was kind to me. Knox was kind, but it had taken him a while to get there so he didn't count. But Eloise and Kira and Zavier and Quinn had been kind from the moment they'd met me. So had Whil, Nova, and Deacon.

There wasn't something fundamentally wrong with me even though I couldn't shift. There was something fundamentally wrong with my old pack, especially my old alpha, his son, and their friends.

Everyone else in the pack I might be able to excuse for their lack of kindness and support because they were afraid. But the others had no excuse. They were cruel because they were horrible, heartless people.

I could see that now.

Bishop and the others had shown me time and again that I was more than what Merrick and Sterling had said I was and that there were people out there who we kind and caring even to strangers.

Perhaps other things were a lie, too.

Perhaps I *could* trust my happiness. Or rather the happiness I'd have once we saved Bishop.

At lunch, we stopped long enough for everyone to eat some rations and for Deacon and Cyrus to switch duties.

Thankfully, I hadn't been watching when Deacon yanked off his kilt and shifted or when Cyrus shifted into his human form and pulled on his clothes. It was safer if I only ogled my mates. Two was good enough for me. It was two more than I ever expected I'd have.

Cyrus stepped close and grabbed the cart's handles, his power stuttering in and out of his control, sending shocking zaps rushing through my body and drawing my attention.

Knox grunted, but he wasn't in any position to complain about his brother's lack of control. His power was a constant, grating vibration against my skin, and even if I hadn't been able to sense the turmoil raging inside him, I would have known keeping it contained to a low steady stream was the best he could manage.

"Hey." I sat up and wrapped my hands around his hand that still clutched tightly to Bishop's and tried to focus on steadying his soul by pushing strength and love through our bond.

We traveled all day, needing to give Bishop six elixirs to stop his convulsions, which was two more than yesterday, and reached the roadside shelter late in the afternoon.

It had a similar construction to the first one with a heavy iron gate, a wide open area scattered with the stone circles indicating fire pits as well as a rocky overhang protecting half the space. At the back was another squat stone building with a metal door and two windows framed by metal shutters.

Cyrus again pulled the cart under the overhang to protect us from any nighttime rain as Deacon in his wolf form, stepped into the mouth of the sheltered area with a small, deer-like creature in his jaws. It looked like he'd already hunted down our dinner while he'd been scouting ahead.

"Good," Cyrus said as he locked the cart in position. "That'll be enough for dinner and breakfast. We can leave the leftovers in the cold cupboard in the shelter for when we come back. I'll get these guys set up and then meet you outside the shelter to help you butcher it."

Cyrus strode around to the back of the cart and held out his hands to me.

"Last time I'll force you to do this," he said, his voice gruff. "But I'll expect you to say something if you're struggling to keep up."

I slid my butt to the edge of the cart, my eyes flickering to his on their own volition.

His expression was strange. It wasn't angry or hard like it usually was, but it was tight with tension mixed with something softer, something heartbreaking.

"I will," I murmured back, that thing in my soul urging me to get closer, to comfort his soul as well. He was just as worried about his brothers as I was... and he was mine.

No. Not mine. Never mine, and I had to pull myself together and stop thinking those kinds of things so I didn't accidentally trap him in a mating bond.

I gritted my teeth and leaned into his embrace so he could lift me off the cart. One arm hooked under my thighs, the other behind my back, and his powerful deep earthy scent enveloped me. Warmth and certainty blossomed around my heart, sending a surge of panic shooting through me.

Not. Mine.

I squeezed my eyes shut until he set me on the ground. But as soon as I opened them, they instantly jumped back to Cyrus and the hurt in his eyes.

Then his alpha-in-control mask snapped into place, leaving me wondering what the hell had just happened.

Except I didn't have the mental strength to figure it out right now. Everything within me was focused on sending assurance and calm to Knox while ignoring the sharp flashes of agony coming through my bond with Bishop. Which was something I wasn't going to outwardly react to because it would make it even harder for Knox to stay in control and Cyrus would question my ability to keep up.

And I was damn well going to keep up.

There were only three or four days left to get to the pool. I'd hiked for a lot longer while fighting my heat. I could do this while fighting the onslaught of overwhelming emotions and a little pain.

AUDREY

For the first day, I was right. I'd woken after a fitful night where we'd had to give Bishop three elixirs, disappointed that I hadn't had another sexy shared dream with my mates and worried for both of them.

Despite that, I'd felt strong and determined, ready to save Bishop. It was as if a glimmer of Knox's powerful feral nature, the strength he'd lent me to stand my ground against Cyrus, had sparked to life inside me. My foot had still been a little tender, but I wasn't going to complain about it because... I. Could. Do. This.

We'd left the cart in the shelter, secured the metal gate to keep out beasts, and marched down the road until midmorning where there was a break in the rocks and a steep, but manageable, slope up into the forest.

Then we'd hiked across the rocky, uneven ground just like we had on our journey north until dusk and set up camp.

Cyrus had commanded I go with Deacon to fill our canteens while Deacon gathered firewood and I'd hopped to it, surprised my legs were barely sore when the last time I'd hiked across the wilderness they'd started to hurt before lunch on the first day.

The next morning, however, was a different story.

I'd gotten even less sleep with Bishop's pain growing stronger inside me and his body twitching and shaking all night despite giving him four elixirs. Knox's worry and rage were also building, crushing inside me, making it difficult to draw in a full breath, *and* I hadn't gotten another sexy dream!

It was ridiculous to be upset about that. Everyone was too stressed to think, or even dream, about sex and yet my soul now ached with need.

God, what was wrong with me?

I bit back a groan, determined to not draw Cyrus's attention, and stretched my achy muscles.

There was nothing wrong with me. I had an incomplete mating bond and just like the last time, it didn't give me any time to adjust. I needed to seal my bond and I needed it now.

Swell.

"All right, ladies," Deacon said as he doused the fire. "Ready for another day? Or do I need to carry you?" The laugh lines at the edges of his eyes crinkled and he flashed us a bright smile.

"I'll be good to get to the pool," Whil replied, rolling

up her blanket and securing it in her pack. "I'm using a bit of magic to fortify my body."

Panic and rage exploded through my bond with Knox, stealing my breath.

"You're wasting magic?" he roared, his eyes going completely black as his wolf took over. "You need your magic to save Bishop."

Whil raised her hands in defense and Deacon stepped in front of her, blocking Knox from getting to her.

"Knox," I gasped, grabbing his arm and pushing as much of my body against his as I could, trying to get him to calm down.

He growled at Deacon, and his claws and canines extended as the feralness within him surged.

Oh, shit. This wasn't good. We were so close. He couldn't lose it now. If he went feral, he could kill Bishop's only hope of survival.

"Stop." My pulse *thu-thudded* hard, and that spark of power exploded from my body, sudden and sharp and gone just as quickly as it appeared.

Knox froze, every muscle in his body tightening, and his claws and canines retracted. He turned his attention to me, his eyes still dark with his wolf.

"It's three more days at most," I murmured, pushing love through our bond.

"He's in agony," his wolf growled at me.

"I know."

He stared at me, his body trembling with his raging

emotions, emotions that threatened my grip on myself. But I rode the violent waves, waiting for his wolf to realize the truth. He couldn't protect Knox from the next three days. If he took control and gave in to his primal fear it was all over.

And it couldn't be over. I needed both of them sane and conscious, not surviving on pure animalistic instinct. My reasons for needing Knox and his wolf hadn't changed since I'd pulled them back from the brink of feralness. I needed his wolf to show me how to be strong and I needed Knox's fierce love.

He'd completely changed after Sterling had tricked me into hurting myself, and I could feel his commitment to me and our bond — even if it was barely noticeable underneath all the other emotions right now. He was my ferocious protector. He didn't care about politics or other people's feelings. If I was in trouble, he'd do whatever it took to protect me. His wolf would, too.

Which was why I didn't push, didn't make his wolf think I was attacking him. I stayed stalwart in my certainty in us, praying that would anchor him back in his body.

And slowly, after an agonizingly long moment of just holding all his emotions without trying to change them, his wolf reached through our bond and found my reasons.

"Whil would never jeopardize Bishop," I soothed as the blackness faded from his eyes, revealing dark brown orbs flecked with brilliant green.

"I know that," he gritted out. "It's just so hard to focus and he's getting worse."

I offered him a soft smile, praying it looked hopeful and he didn't notice just how worried I was about Bishop. "He has us. He's strong. Just three more days."

A burst of Bishop's pain shot through my chest, but I kept my smile soft and breathed through it, determined not to let anyone see how much I was struggling.

I had to be strong for the both of them, and I would be.

"Well then," Deacon said, putting his hands on his hips. "What the hell are we waiting for?"

"That's what I want to know." Cyrus huffed, hooking the now-clean cooking pot to his pack.

"We were waiting for you," Whil said to Cyrus.

"Yeah," Deacon replied. "You need to volunteer more in the kitchen. How long does it take to wash a pot and a couple of bowls?"

CYRUS

I rolled my eyes at Deacon, praying he wouldn't notice the real reason I took five times longer to wash the pot and bowls than usual, and started marching toward the pool assuming everyone else would follow. I'd tried to shift out the evidence, but Deacon had a sensitive nose that he liked to stick in other people's business and he wasn't as distracted by Bishop's condition as Knox was.

Jeez. This was what I'd become. It was like I was a pup again, hiding in the mountains to jerk off so no one knew.

But early this morning, while I was sitting on watch, Audrey's scent had started to change. Her sweet fresh scent had deepened with desire even while she was unconscious and my wolf had lost it.

He wasn't going to let Audrey suffer through another heat fever and he was determined to stop it before it even started... despite the fact that her changing scent might not indicate another heat and could just be her incomplete mating bond compelling her to seal it.

As it was, I'd escaped camp with the morning dishes, praying no one had noticed my cock tenting my pants, washed the dishes as fast as I could, and then shucked my clothes — since I couldn't afford to have them smell like my arousal.

With a groan, I'd fallen to my knees and grabbed myself. My cock was already painfully hard and leaking precum thanks to my wolf's eagerness to claim Audrey and the realization that maybe, one day, I could.

That crack in my determination to never mate with her had been enough for him to take a little more control of our body. Thankfully, that crack wasn't enough for him to come on to Audrey — we both knew that wouldn't go over well given the current situation — but it was enough to make me need a release.

I huffed a bitter laugh.

I was just kidding myself. I didn't need my wolf to make me hard for Audrey. I hadn't even needed to see her glorious and radiating alpha power to defy me. I'd wanted her from the moment I'd seen her, a small, broken warrior defying death himself.

But I'd just been so determined to do right by my pack.

Except my pack would eventually come around and I'd expel any from the pack who wanted to hurt her. I just needed to be patient, needed to find the right moment where my pack would accept her and she'd accept me as her mate.

I squeezed my cock, knowing the only way to get it to calm down was to come, and my thoughts had jumped to our one time together. It had been terrifying and heart-breaking, and I hadn't been able to stop thinking about it, about how tight she was, how warm, how fragile. I'd needed to protect her, care for her, love her, and that feeling had only grown stronger the more I tried to avoid her.

I'd roughly jerked my hand along my length until hot jets of cum had poured into the stream where I'd washed the pots. Then I shifted into my wolf and back to human, destroying the scent of my cum as much as possible.

Now I was hiking downwind of her — because that was the direction we had to go — her scent pure torture and pure ecstasy as each tiny gust dragged it over me.

"We need to pick up our pace," Deacon said, his voice low, as he stepped up beside me.

His attention flickered back to the others behind us and his expression turned serious. "You can smell that, can't you? Audrey's need? It's subtle, but it's there."

"You think it's subtle?" I choked out. I was damn near drowning in it.

He glanced down at my crotch where I'd secured my hard-as-hell cock under the waistband of my pants so my condition wasn't so obvious — and something I'd needed to do less than ten minutes after jerking off.

"Ah," he said, that one word filled with knowing.

"Nova would say you're hyper-attuned to her scent after watching her suffer through a heat fever for so long."

"What would you say?" I wasn't sure I wanted to know, but he was a good friend and my beta. He knew the whole situation and wouldn't let his friendship with Audrey get in the way of telling me the truth. I trusted him, even if I looked like an idiot.

"That it's too soon for Audrey's incomplete bond to start affecting her and we need to save Bishop and get them to bond before it's more than just a little desire. Oh, and—" He flashed me a crooked smile, his eyes bright with laughter even as he managed to keep it in and not laugh out loud. "Nova's right."

"Not always," I huffed.

He cocked an eyebrow at me. "Nova is always right."

Yeah, Nova was wrong so few times it didn't count.

"I think your instincts are telling you something about Audrey, but you've made a royal mess of it before it could even get started."

"The pack needs to accept her first," I insisted. "I won't put her through that scrutiny and hate."

"She's stronger than you think she is," Deacon replied.

"No," I corrected. "She's stronger than *she* thinks she is, and I won't put her in front of the pack as my mate until she realizes that. I won't be cruel to her."

"Again," Deacon said, the laughter melting from his eyes, his expression turning serious. "You won't be cruel to her *again*."

"Yeah." I ran my hands over my head, fearing the damage was already done. Putting her in front of my pack as my mate was pure fantasy. It meant she'd have to accept me first, and I wasn't sure I'd ever be able to convince her that her heart, not just her body, was safe with me.

KNOX

MY INSIDES WERE A SUFFOCATING TWISTED KNOT. WE WERE going too fucking slow. And yet that thought twisted me up even more because faster meant more strain on Audrey. She was keeping up — because my mate was strong — but I feared it wouldn't last. Even the strongest shifter could break with enough stress and she was under so much.

And I could still feel her stress despite my wolf freaking out while I fought the threatening feralness inside me.

She was fighting to be strong for me, sending a near-constant stream of love and determination through our bond, but the emotions were edged with fear. A fear I couldn't do anything about because I couldn't shut off my most primal nature and get my emotions under control.

I was also pretty sure she was feeling some of Bishop's agony. She didn't seem to be experiencing the constant stream of pain slicing into her soul like I was, but I saw her flinch whenever the pain surged. And on top of that, her scent had changed, deepening with need like when she'd first started fighting her heat before we'd even left Stonehaven to go north.

Back then, it had been her incomplete bond with me setting her off, so I was certain it was her bond with Bishop doing the same thing now.

Her scent, however, hadn't changed this quickly before. Her bond with Bishop was less than a day old, and I feared she was going to have a heat fever again, possibly before we even reached the pool.

All of which she was trying to hide from me because she didn't want me to worry.

Except all I could do was worry, since I couldn't hold both her and Bishop, and I *had* to hold Bishop. His soul was the weakest right now, and if I let go for too long, I'd lose him.

As if thinking about losing him to the poison gave it strength, agony burst through my twin bond, blacking out my vision for a second. Bishop moaned and tensed, the precursor to a convulsion.

"Whil," I growled, and she pulled out an elixir without me having to say more while I had to watch Audrey stumble and couldn't do anything to help her.

"Shit," Cyrus hissed, grabbing her before she fell, his body almost as stiff as Bishop's.

His nose twitched and his eyes squeezed shut for a

moment, but Audrey didn't notice, her worried expression locked on Bishop.

So, he could smell it, too.

Was it as potent to him as it was to me? Was her need so strong because I was attuned to her and was partially feeling it through our bond, or could everyone smell her?

A growl bubbled in the back of my throat.

Mine.

She was mine, and my wolf didn't want anyone else to know she needed sex, especially when I couldn't satisfy her right this minute.

"We have enough elixirs to make it to the pool," Whil said, mistaking my growl for worry for Bishop. "I'm not letting him die."

I huffed and gave her a tight nod, the pressure and wildness inside me squeezing so tight I could barely breathe.

Audrey took a big step away from Cyrus, her cheeks just a little too pink. "I can make it to our next camp without stopping for lunch. How about you, Whil?"

"No," Cyrus barked with a snap of power that made Audrey tense. "Neither of you can hike on two meals a day. I won't have you slowing us down because you're hungry." His power stuttered again, slipping out of his control, and Audrey squared her shoulders and glared at him.

"It's only three days. I've survived worse for longer."

More power snapped from Cyrus and my wolf growled.

She'd suffered without food for longer than three days?

If her previous alpha wasn't already dead, and I could get to her realm — which I couldn't — I'd kill him for making her suffer.

"I doubt you were also exerting yourself at the same time."

"And we're losing time arguing about it," Deacon said with a snap of his power, what little control he had also slipping.

My wolf seized our body and I jerked forward. "Mine."

Deacon's eyes widened and more power snapped from him. He threw his hands up and backed away from Audrey even though he wasn't even close to her.

"Yours," Audrey assured my wolf, wrapping her hands around my biceps. "Always yours."

Love flooded our bond, easing the crushing tension in my chest, and I nearly dropped to my knees with relief.

"But Deacon's right," she added, looking exhausted for a split second before her sweet, soft smile returned. "We have to keep moving."

"And you have to eat," Cyrus insisted as he started walking at a fast pace.

"I'll eat and walk," she shot back.

"You'll choke," he growled.

"I won't choke."

He shot her a hard glare. "You tripped over nothing on the completely flat death god's lands. I'll just consider it a miracle if we get to the pool without you breaking something."

"The rest of the way to and from the death god's lands was just as rocky as here." She swept out her hand, gesturing at the rocky, uneven landscape.

Trees, thick with leaves, as well as evergreens, crowded close, creating a thick cool shade, blocking the summer's heat, but that also made the jagged landscape and fallen trees slippery with moss and rot.

"You *just* tripped." He jerked his thumb over his shoulder to where we'd stopped a moment ago.

"Bishop was about to convulse. I was distracted," she huffed. Then her eyes widened and a new worry trembled through our bond. "I'll stop long enough to eat a granola bar and an apple."

What the fuck? Why the hell had she just submitted to him?

The worry quickly turned into frustration as if she were angry at herself for not standing her ground.

"A wise wolf knows how to pick her battles," Deacon whispered to her even though both Cyrus and I could easily hear him. "He's too stubborn to see sense right now. There's no point going up against that brick wall unless it's absolutely necessary. Stopping for a quick snack is a good compromise. Well done."

Surprise and pleasure leaped through our mating bond, and she dropped her gaze to her feet, her cheeks turning pink again.

For a second, I thought she was reciprocating

Deacon's flirtations until I realized she was actually reacting to his praise.

She practically lit up at a simple well done. Of course, if I praised her, it would come out all wrong. That didn't mean I wasn't going to try, but the best mate for that was Bishop and I was sure as hell telling him that little fact about Audrey.

I'd make sure he praised her as much as he told her she was beautiful. We just needed to get to the damned pool first.

AUDREY

A COUPLE OF HOURS LATER, I WAS STILL RIDING THE HIGH of Deacon's simple "well done" when we stopped for our lunchtime snack. Whil and I ate as fast as possible so we could keep moving while Knox clung to a now-constantly trembling and moaning Bishop. Deacon tried to lighten the mood with funny stories about growing up in the pack with Nova and the guys — even though he was more than fifteen years older than the twins — and Cyrus spent the time glaring into the forest.

A part of me was furious at myself for realizing that I'd been talking back to Cyrus and had gotten nervous, while another part was furious that I'd submitted to his wishes without much of a fight, my fear of angry alphas raising its ugly head once again.

I'd thought I was doing better. I'd been worried about his reaction to me while we traveled, but not afraid that he'd yell at me like he had in the arena. There were even times when I felt comfortable with him, that sense of trust deep within me overriding all common sense.

Not to mention, he had to be under horrible stress. I was kind of surprised he hadn't yelled at me yet. Sure, he'd huffed at me to do things, but he hadn't cracked like he had in the arena when Knox was about to go completely feral, and he wasn't giving me the cold shoulder. A lukewarm shoulder, but that was a big improvement from before.

Although I still got the impression that he didn't want to talk to me. That, however, I could live with, especially since I needed to keep my distance from him. I didn't want to accidentally mate bond with him despite that strange part inside me insisting I needed more, that he was mine like Bishop and Knox were.

We hiked until after dusk and found a cave where we'd be out of the elements. So far, the weather had been perfect, but that didn't mean it would stay that way.

Knox had told me the summer was their stormy season when violent storms suddenly appeared from magic that had built up over the resting places of a couple of storm gods.

The cave would also protect us from beasts, although they, too, hadn't been a bother. I hadn't even really sensed their presence like I had on the journey north.

But, as Deacon explained, the pack regularly hunted the most dangerous beasts in the area around the road to keep the trade route open as well as around the pool to protect those guarding and tending to it.

The Kingdom of Lais considered the pool a sacred resource that needed to be nurtured and protected, especially since Whil could create powerful healing elixirs from its water, and the pack and kingdom had strengthened their once weak alliance because of it. All of which could fall apart if something happened to the pool.

"Deacon, dinner," Cyrus commanded, setting down his pack as Knox sat at the mouth of the cave with Bishop — which was as deep into the cave as he could go without setting off his claustrophobia. "Audrey, grab the canteens and stick by me while I gather firewood."

"I'm not going to trip," I mumbled under my breath, setting my pack beside Knox's and brushing my lips across his in a quick, reassuring kiss.

Except that was a mistake, and the whisper of our lips touching made need swell low within me.

Knox's eyes darkened while his expression turned pained, and I tried to focus on anything other than sex. I wasn't nearly as needy as I'd been last time... but it had only been two days since I'd formed my incomplete bond with Bishop and my desire had been steadily growing despite being hungry and tired and worried.

"Of course you're going to trip," Cyrus replied, having heard me with his god-damned wolf-enhanced hearing. "It's after dark and you don't have night vision. I'd tell you to stay here but—"

But Knox couldn't leave Bishop and Whil was better at sensing the magical poison and knowing when it was time for another elixir. Whoever was gathering the firewood might have been able to fill the canteens as well, but everything was faster with more people helping.

I grabbed the canteens and followed Cyrus out into the darkness where he led me to a river. Unlike when we set up camp going north and pretty much followed the river the whole way there, this river was farther away. I doubted we were within screaming distance of the camp even with Knox's enhanced hearing and there was no way I'd have been able to find it myself.

I also didn't want to admit that there was a good chance I'd have tripped and hurt myself on the way here if Cyrus hadn't been with me.

With the exception of a glade at the bottom of a steep ridge, the trees had crowded close, blocking out the moonlight, and there'd been a few terrifying moments when I'd been almost blind and nearly lost my footing. But I did successfully get to the river without tripping.

One point for me.

None for the grumpy overbearing — far too sexy — alpha.

Shoving that thought to the back of my mind, I filled the canteens while Cyrus gathered firewood.

My desire for him was just the desire from my incomplete mating bond that was making me more attracted to him than I was.

Except I knew that wasn't true, and every time I tried to pretend I wasn't aware of his powerful body nearby or how he'd helped me navigate the uneven ground in the darkness, that stupid fantasy flashed through my mind.

Cyrus holding me, pushing into me, and kissing me like I meant something to him. Like I was precious and wanted and—

Stop. Just stop.

"You done?" Cyrus asked, making me jump.

Shit. I'd been so caught up in the fantasy — and denying the fantasy — that I hadn't heard him approach.

"Ah..." I pulled the canteen I was holding from the water, secured the lid, and reached to grab the next one.

Except all the lids were screwed on. They'd all been open when I'd reached the river, so somehow I'd filled the canteens while daydreaming and hadn't even noticed.

Jeez. I hadn't been this distracted by my heat when we'd traveled north. Of course, I also hadn't been under this much stress. My body ached for a release and I was crazy frustrated that I stopped having sex dreams with my mates. On top of it, I was terrified I was going to lose both Bishop and Knox but had to stay calm to keep Knox from going feral.

I should probably be surprised I wasn't a sobbing mess by now. Getting distracted from a sexy fantasy that was never going to happen was the least of my worries.

"Come on," he said, his voice gruff. He jerked his chin the way we'd come, his hands full of firewood, and started leading the way back.

I followed, weighed down by the now-full canteens, and carefully picked my way across the uneven ground, my pace so slow Cyrus kept stopping to gather more fire-wood, not so subtly waiting for me to catch up. But I was determined not to trip and with my hands full, it wasn't as easy to catch myself if I lost my balance.

We climbed up a shallow slope, rounded a tall chunk of rock jutting up from the ground, and stepped onto the ridge overlooking the glade.

Moonlight filled the glade, illuminating our path, and I breathed a quick sigh of relief. We still had three-quarters of the way to get back to camp, but at least for this stretch, I wouldn't have to worry about not seeing where I was going.

I picked up my pace, eager to catch up to Cyrus who stood at the center of the ridge, waiting for me. But I'd only managed to get halfway to him when the ground gave way beneath me.

With a yelp, I lurched to the side and knew I couldn't save myself. I was rolling down that steep incline to the bottom whether I wanted to or not.

Cyrus's eyes flashed wide, realization hitting him, and he dropped his firewood and lunged at me, grabbing my wrist.

But it was already too late. My fall was inevitable and he had to stretch to reach me, throwing him off balance, too.

Together, we tumbled over the edge, crashing through small shrubs and over hunks of stone, the world spinning around me so fast I had no idea which way was up or down.

We landed with a heavy thump, heaped together at the bottom on a cushion of moss and fallen leaves. Somehow, Cyrus had managed to pull me to his chest and turn so I ended on top of him with his hard body wrapped protectively around mine.

Mine, that annoying little voice in my head whispered as a surge of desire swept through me.

I scrambled off him, falling onto my butt and bashing my elbow on a tree trunk. This was *not* the way tonight was supposed to go. I was supposed to have proven to Cyrus that I wasn't a klutz and not ended up in his embrace.

"Damn it," I huffed, slapping the ground with my frustration. "I was determined I wasn't going to trip."

Cyrus huffed back — it almost sounded like a laugh. "Rest assured, you didn't trip. The ground gave out beneath you. Obviously not your fault."

I rolled my eyes at him, surprised he pointed out the difference. "Are you sure? You're not one to sugarcoat anything."

"You're not a disaster, Audrey." He leaned forward, his moss green eyes locked on mine as he plucked a leaf out of my hair.

Except he didn't lean back when he was done.

The heat from his body teased across my skin. He was close. Too close. And yet I didn't have the willpower to put space between us.

Except I *had* to put space between us.

The ache between my legs was growing stronger every second I was captured in his gaze, and that awful voice was getting louder.

Not mine. Never mine, I insisted. I couldn't accidentally trap him in a mating bond.

"But you scared the shit out of me," he confessed, reaching and pulling another leaf from my hair, the motion drawing him even closer.

So close that if I dipped forward, our lips would touch.

I squeezed my eyes shut, trying to think of something else, anything else. But it was like I could feel his alpha power caressing inside me, not with a command, but a plea. I wasn't even sure he was aware he was doing it.

"Audrey," he breathed. "Are you hurt?"

"I'm fine," I immediately replied.

"Audrey." He captured my chin with his hand.

My eyes flew open at the sudden contact and I was caught in his gaze again. He was commanding and strong, his alpha power rolling off him in soft, almost teasing waves that made all of me tingle. He was the most powerful member of his pack, the ideal mate, and that made the stupid primal something inside me giddy from his attention.

Which was stupid stupid stupid.

He didn't want me and I didn't want someone who didn't want me.

It was bad enough when Knox had frozen our mating bond and nearly broken my spirit. Cyrus would crush me, probably without even trying.

"Are you hurt?" he asked again.

This time I dragged my attention away from him and

focused on my body, that stupid primal nature wanting to please him.

Nothing hurt bad enough to be worried about it. I'd gathered a few new bruises and scrapes but that was all.

"Just a little beaten up. I can make it to the pools."

A low growl bubbled in Cyrus's throat and he captured my head between his palms. "That wasn't what I was asking about. I'd have happily carried you to the pools all the way from Stonehaven. I'm worried about *you*."

"I'm not going to die and endanger your brothers."

The growl came out in full, the sound vibrating through my body and sending more heat rushing to my core instead of scaring me.

"Not worried about that, either, Audrey," he rumbled. "This, here and now, is all about you. My worry is all about you. No one else."

"Me?" I squeaked, his words sending me spinning while making something in my heart swell.

I had to be unconscious and dreaming. Cyrus's worry had always been about my connection to his brothers... or had I just assumed that?

"I—" I didn't know what to say. "I—"

"You, Audrey," he insisted and dipped forward, capturing my mouth in a searing, breathtaking kiss.

AUDREY

HOT ACHING NEED EXPLODED IN MY CORE, AND I GRABBED the front of Cyrus's shirt and kissed him back. All the reasons I had for keeping my distance from him vanished.

Except they'd been good reasons.

They'd been...

What had they been?

He tangled his fingers in my hair and deepened the kiss, his tongue battling with mine, his free hand still carefully cupping my cheek. It was just like the fantasy I'd been having of him from the moment I'd woken from my heat fever.

Cyrus held me as if I were precious, like he loved me, but this time the kiss wasn't soft and sweet, it was deep and passionate. Whatever wall he'd locked his heart and all his emotions behind had broken open, turning him into the man I'd hoped he'd be, the man I wanted him to be.

Because he. Was. Mine.

That voice inside me that wanted the impossible howled with joy, and I let it. I didn't care about the consequences—

I mean I did. They were really important. But—

What were they again?

"Audrey," Cyrus groaned, pulling away to look me in the eyes. "You're the most frustrating person I've ever met."

But there wasn't a hint of frustration in his eyes. Instead, they were dark with his wolf and hungry.

Need shivered down my spine and Cyrus sucked in a deep breath, drawing in my scent. The hunger deepened and so did my desire. I ached like I'd ached when I'd been battling my heat, just before I succumbed to a heat fever and lost all awareness.

I'd always been attracted to Cyrus. He was just as handsome as his brothers but edgier. Not dark and brooding like Knox, but fierce and commanding. Everything about him screamed bad boy... or hardened warrior — which was more likely the case.

He made the rules and everyone else obeyed.

And I *wanted* him this very minute in this moonlit glade, cushioned by a soft bed of moss and leaves. Fireflies had even come out, little spots of light dancing around us, making the moment feel magical, and every nerve, every cell in my body, ached for him.

"You don't have to do everything by yourself. There are people around you who want to help. *I* want to help."

And from the longing in his eyes, his "help" was to make me come, screaming his name.

"Yes," I breathed. "Please."

I tightened my grip on his shirt and we crashed back together, kissing as if we needed each other to breathe.

His hands were everywhere, clutching my hair, pushing under my shirt, palming my breasts, sliding into my pants. I arched into his touch, my body begging for him for more as I dragged my hands over him.

I couldn't get enough. He was so strong, so powerful, so stunningly beautiful in his edgy bad boy way. He wasn't loving like Bishop or wild like Knox, but there was something overwhelming about him. He possessed me with his mouth and hands, made me gasp and moan, building up my need until I ached for a release.

"Cyrus," I begged. "I need— I need."

I clawed at his shirt, and he pulled back long enough to grab his collar with one hand and haul it off.

Eagerly, I swept my hands over his chest, savoring the feel of his bulky powerful muscles. I was so small, so fragile compared to him. He could attack me and I wouldn't stand a chance, and yet in this moment, I felt completely safe.

Cyrus would protect me. He'd take care of me. He'd satisfy my needs. He—

There was something wrong about that. He wasn't—? I shouldn't—?

With a groan, he pushed me onto my back and smashed his lips against mine, his tongue demanding entrance.

My desire surged and my thoughts scattered.

Yes. Yes more. I needed this. Needed him.

Needed to relieve the pressure building up inside me before I went insane.

I clawed at his back and bucked my hips up, hitting his erection and making him growl. His gaze darkened with desire, sending shivers of need rushing through me, and I bucked up again, showing him with my body what I needed.

Except instead of grinding down against me or yanking down my pants, he frowned.

There was something I was supposed to remember—

But the emotion disappeared as quickly as it appeared and he shoved his hand down the front of my pants, once again scattering my thoughts.

Oh, yes. This was what I wanted.

Two of his fingers swept through my folds and plunged inside me, and I moaned my pleasure.

Thank God he wasn't going to tease me. I didn't think I'd survive if he wanted to draw this out.

I rolled my hips, taking his fingers deep within me, savoring the feel of them driving into me hard and fast, setting every nerve on fire.

In seconds, I lit up and screamed his name. Pleasure roared through me and I didn't care that I'd come so quickly. Quickly meant he'd plunge his cock inside me sooner, and his cock was what I really wanted, what I needed to break the desire threatening to burn me up.

"Yes," I moaned. "More." More more more.

I rose up and kissed him but instead of returning the kiss, he jerked back, and gave his head a hard shake.

What the—?

"Cyrus?" My throat tightened.

Why wasn't he—?

Because this is wrong, a tiny voice in the back of my mind said, barely audible against the roar of my desire.

Not wrong, that strange wildness inside me roared back. *Mine.*

"Fuck, Audrey. No. I'm sorry." He drew back even farther, sucked in deep breaths as if to steady himself, and ran his hands through his hair, not seeming to care that he had my cum all over his fingers. "This isn't us."

Mine.

Except something about his words rang true, like I agreed with them despite desperately needing him.

I squeezed my eyes shut.

The voice inside me that claimed he was mine had always been wrong. He wasn't mine and wasn't interested in being mine, except...

God, why was it so hard to think?

He cupped my cheeks, his touch making my eyes fly open, and I was drowning in the heat and hunger in his gaze.

"We're being influenced by spirits," he forced out, worry seeping into his desire.

"Spirits?"

That didn't make sense. I'd wanted him before this moment... but I'd never have acted on it.

Oh, shit.

One of the fireflies zipped close, drawing my attention, and I stared at it, stunned, unable to understand what I was looking at.

It wasn't a firefly.

It was a fairy — the kind from fairy tales, not the fae who'd come to earth to join the fight against Michael. The little creature screeched at us and tossed a surprisingly large handful of glitter with its tiny hands.

I gasped in surprise and the glitter caught in the back of my throat and up my nose.

"No, Audrey," Cyrus said, jerking me forward.

Except instead of protecting me from the spirit, his lips crashed against mine again.

Oh, yes. Yes yes yes.

Now we could finish what we'd started.

I ran my hands down Cyrus's muscular chest, from his pecs and the rippling female fantasy of his abs to the waistband of his pants.

"Audrey," he groaned. "Fuck, I want you. I've wanted —" He jerked away, the muscles in his jaw flexing as he fought the fairy's magic.

"I want you, too." And I did, but...

He didn't really want me. He'd made that clear.

The spirits. Damn it.

Another fairy darted toward us and I slapped it away.

We had to get out of there. It was bad enough that Cyrus had kissed the hell out of me and made me come with his fingers. We couldn't let it go to the next step.

I could accidentally mate bond with him.

That was it! That was what I'd been forgetting!

I didn't want to trap him in a mating bond.

AUDREY

"Cyrus!" I shoved him back, catching him by surprise — since that was the only way I'd be able to move him. "We have to get out of here."

His body tensed and his eyes squeezed shut then they flew open and captured me. They were black. His wolf was in control and he wanted me.

I froze, knowing if I made a move, he'd think I was fleeing and pounce.

Two more fairies buzzed around us, and his face partially shifted into a snout. He snapped at the spirits, devouring them with a desperate, high-pitched scream and a stomach-churning crunch.

"Mine," he snarled.

"Not yours," I forced out, the words tearing something in my soul.

He doesn't want me. He doesn't want me. He doesn't want me.

And yet I ached for him, body, heart, and soul. I was incomplete without him, just like I'd been incomplete without Knox and Bishop.

No. That was the fairy glitter speaking. It wasn't true.

I should be God damned happy with the two mates I already had.

"Cyrus." This time I barked the words, my pulse *thu-thudding*, and he jerked back as if I'd slapped him. "We have to get out of here."

If we didn't leave now, whatever hold I had on myself would shatter, and I'd succumb to my glitter-induced desire.

He grabbed me, stood, and tossed me over his shoulder.

With his free hand, he slapped two more spirits out of the air before rushing to the rise we'd fallen down.

The fairies screeched as he scrambled up the rise and tossed more glitter at us. For a second, I was surrounded in a thick cloud of glitter, the grit rushing up my nose and into my mouth and making my eyes water.

I *loved* Cyrus. I *needed* Cyrus.

My desire turned to lava, pouring through my veins. I couldn't breathe, couldn't think. I *needed*. Oh, God, I needed him.

I squirmed in his grip. "Cyrus," I begged.

He crested the ridge and set me on the ground where I promptly yanked off my shirt.

"Audrey—"

I grabbed my breasts, desperate for relief, but pleasuring myself wasn't what I wanted. I wanted Cyrus. We belonged together.

He. Was. Mine.

"I need you," I pleaded. "Please." I rose on my knees and grabbed the waistband of his pants.

"It's the spirits' magic," he said, his voice gruff as he grabbed my wrists, stopping me from undoing his pants.

"I know it is." God, I knew he didn't want me and that I wasn't in love with him, and yet that small voice of reason in the back of my mind was being devoured by my need. "Please. I love you."

He crouched, still holding my wrists. "You don't love me. That's the spirits," he said, his expression strained.

My eyes burned with tears that I didn't want to cry, but his rejection was breaking my heart.

This was ridiculous. I didn't love him. I was still partially afraid of him.

And yet...

And yet it felt as if there was truth in those words. How long had the niggling voice in the back of my mind been telling me he was mine?

My desire flared, stealing my breath and arching my back. My breasts were so heavy, needy, and I'd soaked through my pants.

"Audrey." He cupped my cheeks, urging me to look at him. "This isn't a fever. You're not hot. We'll get you to Knox and—"

Another jolt of desire twisted me tight.

"Look at me, Audrey," he commanded.

I dragged my eyes open, not realizing I'd closed them.

"The magic will wear off but— Fuck." His expression turned pained. "I'll get you off again and then get you to Knox."

"Where everyone will watch us have sex," I told him. Sure I'd liked it when Knox had watched me have sex with Bishop and vice versa, but Deacon and Whil...?

The thought made my stomach churn. I had to have sex now and it had to be with Cyrus.

God, what was wrong with me? Why was I so adamant to have Cyrus relieve my need? "Why won't you have sex with me?"

The words came out choked and tears leaked from my eyes.

"You're being influenced by magic." He gathered me in his arms and cradled me against his chest, the sensation so comforting, so right... so... familiar.

I gasped, drawing back so I could look him in the eyes. "We've had sex before. It wasn't a fantasy. It really happened."

"You were dying and Bishop couldn't—" The muscles in his jaw flexed. "It was just your heat. It didn't mean anything."

"And it doesn't mean anything now," I lied. "This fairy glitter isn't easing up. Every time I move or twitch, or hell, even breathe, I ache. I can't take it anymore and we both know if Knox saw me like this he'd lose his shit."

"He's going to lose his shit over me having sex with

you," Cyrus huffed as he helped me stand and slid my pants off my hips and down my legs.

With a groan, he grabbed my waist and drew me close, pressing his nose into my curls and drawing in deep breaths.

That wasn't the action of a man who didn't want to make love to me.

Except he'd also been affected by the spirits' magic. He might not have gotten that final, enormous face full that I had, but he'd still been dosed enough to kiss me like he loved me and make me come.

I had to keep remembering that.

And I *had* to keep remembering that this was just the same situation as my heat fever. I needed someone to fuck me and he was the only one present who could.

Another tear trailed down my cheek, and I tipped my head back just in case Cyrus looked up.

He nuzzled lower, sending shivers rushing down my spine, then flicked his tongue against my clit.

Sensation zinged through me, tensing my muscles then melting them with liquid need. Now I wasn't holding my head back to keep him from seeing my tears, it was thrown back in ecstasy.

He flicked again and again, and more shivers rolled down my body. I was already so worked up that a few more flicks had me coming.

I let out a long, satisfied moan as hot relief flooded my body and leaked from between my thighs.

Cyrus clutched me tight as I rode the wave, bliss washing through me, languid and hot.

But the ache returned, urging me to squirm, pressed my breasts into his face, or even push him back down to lick me clean.

"Damn it," I hissed. Not that I expected a quick little orgasm like that to bleed off the spirits' magic.

"I've got you," he murmured, just like when he'd helped me with my heat. "I've got you."

He undid his pants and pushed them to his knees, before pulling me down to straddle him.

My hips rocked forward, eager for more, painting my release over his large cock.

So big. Larger than Knox and Bishop. And I had to still be under the spirits' influence because that didn't scare me at all. Instead, it made more need rush from my core.

Everything within me screamed to take him. Take him now. I needed to be filled by him, loved by him, because he was mine.

He kissed me tenderly, like how he'd kissed me in my fantasy— No, not my fantasy. When we'd had sex during my heat. And my heart broke a little more.

It doesn't mean anything to him.

And I still needed him with my heart, my essence, my very soul.

I forced those thoughts from my head and gave into the lusty haze from the glitter. I grabbed his cock between us, spreading around my release, not needing to do anything to work him up. He was hard as steel and precum wept from his slit. The urge to slide from his lap and take him in my mouth swelled up inside me, but Cyrus held tight with both hands on my hips, his fingers nearly spanning my waist, refusing to let me go.

Then, with a low growl, he lifted me up and eased me down his length slowly, being oh so careful as his girth stretched me to the edge of my limit, verging on painful.

But the spirits' magic didn't care if he was too big for me or if I needed to relax more. The desire surging within me needed to be satisfied.

This was what it wanted. What deep down, *I* wanted.

Possessed by the glitter, I begged for him to go faster, harder, fill me, now. My hips rocked, and I dug my fingernails into his shoulders, straining against his hold on me.

His breath turned as ragged as mine, his control driving me crazy until finally — finally! — our pelvises met and he was completely buried inside me.

"Cyrus," I moaned, rocking my hips, savoring the feel of him. "You feel so good."

My head rolled back and he nuzzled my neck, teasing soft kisses along my jaw, his body trembling... and not moving.

"Cyrus?" Uncertainty wormed its way into the haze. Was he regretting this?

Oh, God. I'd fucked up. I'd fucked up so bad.

Then he grabbed the nape of my neck and braced his other hand behind my back and slowly slid out.

My muscles twitched with pleasure. He felt amazing.

Just like how Knox and Bishop felt. His large cock raked against my channel, igniting already hypersensitive nerves, and sending me spinning.

Carefully, he pushed back in then withdrew. He repeated the process again and again, driving me crazy.

Making love to me.

This wasn't a quick fuck. I could feel the emotion in every stroke, every groan slipping from his lips. He drove me higher and higher, his pace getting faster and faster as he built a glorious peak then sent me flying.

Every muscle in my body clenched, my channel seizing him as he fucked through my orgasm to his own release. With a long low groan, he came hard, clenching me to his body and turning my amazing orgasm into something glorious.

The world went white and I spun around and around, pleasure rushing through me. Tremors rolled aftershock after aftershock through me, capturing me in breath-taking bliss.

Mine. He was mine.

"Maybe one day," Cyrus murmured against my temple, so softly I could barely hear him. "One day."

AUDREY

CYRUS HELD ME AS THE HEAT OF THE GLITTER-INDUCED desire cooled and our breathing returned to normal. "Are you okay?"

I nodded but kept clinging to him, afraid to look him in the eyes. I didn't know what to say or how to feel.

Disappointment and frustration twisted in my gut, and I could only hope Knox was too distracted by his own emotions and Bishop's pain to notice... because I had no idea what to say to him, either.

In the moment, I'd been so sure Cyrus was mine and I had to have him and I sure as hell couldn't have made it back to camp without having sex. But I hadn't formed a mating bond with him, which meant that horrible voice inside me that insisted he was mine was wrong.

And now I had no idea how I could ever look him in the eyes.

Except I was also frustrated that I felt that way. Sure, I was attracted to him and I had fantasies about him — which actually hadn't been fantasies but memories — but that didn't mean there was something between us.

Hell, I still didn't completely trust him despite what my instincts were telling me.

It was exactly what I'd told him before we'd had sex. It didn't mean anything.

He'd been helping me out like he'd helped me out during my heat. We'd both been influenced by the spirits and their magical glitter and it was never going to happen again... no matter how much that stupid voice inside me wanted it.

"Come on," he said as he carefully lifted me off his lap and set me on the ground. "We have to get back to camp."

I grabbed my pants — they were the closest — and stood on shaky legs to put them on.

Inside me, Knox's emotions continued to crush around my heart, adding to my own confusing mix of emotions. I was going to have to talk with him about what had happened. We were mates and I'd had sex with someone else. I wasn't going to try to hide it.

I mentally rolled my eyes at myself. Even if I wanted to — which I didn't because that was wrong — there was no way I'd be able to hide it. I could scrub myself down in the stream where I'd filled our canteens and Knox still would have been able to smell his brother on me.

I finished getting dressed while Cyrus pulled up his

pants and retrieved four of our six canteens scattered across the top of the ridge. The other two, along with his shirt, were at the bottom in the glade, sacrifices to whichever god or goddess of sex or love or whatever slept in the land below.

He handed me the canteens, gathered a large armful of firewood, and we hiked back to camp.

Deacon glanced up, the first to see us, and his eyes widened. "What happened?"

Everyone else looked up at his words and I hunched my shoulders, curling in on myself, not wanting to deal with questions or judgment even among people I considered friends.

"Aphrodite's lands have expanded," Cyrus huffed as if that explained everything. And maybe it did. We'd been overcome with lust and it had been a battle to stop ourselves long enough to get away.

"Are you okay, Audrey?" Deacon asked, his expression growing concerned even as his nostrils flared, not-so-subtly drawing in the scent of mine and Cyrus's mixed releases.

"I'm fine." I set the canteens near our packs and started to sag to the ground beside Bishop, nervous about Knox's reaction.

But before my knees hit the cavern's floor, Knox grabbed me, pulled me into his lap, and clung to me as if he were afraid I was going to run away. "You're not fine."

"I had sex with your brother. I didn't mean to, but I'd wanted to and I..." Guilt twisted in my gut.

"Did he give you what you need?"

I nodded, afraid to speak.

"Then that's all that matters."

Love and certainty cut through the other emotions, and I leaned into him, clinging to the sensation. This time, he was sending me reassurance and I knew in my heart he didn't think I'd done anything wrong. Still, it had been extenuating circumstances and I couldn't let it happen again.

No matter how much that voice in my head was certain Cyrus was mine.

"Once we've saved Bishop, the three of you are going to have to talk about Audrey taking more mates," Cyrus said, his voice gruff as he added more wood to the fire.

"What?" I gasped as Knox tensed and Deacon choked mid-sip of his canteen, spraying water into the flames.

That strange primal feeling inside me jolted as if Cyrus's words confirmed that he was mine even though it was clear he wasn't.

"You couldn't have waited until she bonded with Bishop then gotten Bishop to bring it up," Deacon groaned.

"It's obvious she's feeling guilty," Cyrus shot back. "She needs to get over that or she's going to be in trouble when her next heat hits."

"I'm sure two mates will be more than enough," I insisted, my cheeks burning with embarrassment.

The muscles in Cyrus's jaw flexed. "You need to prepare yourself. You formed mating bonds with Knox and Bishop without the vows and your last heat turned into a near-deadly fever just like a powerful female alpha without enough mates."

"That was because of my incomplete mating bond. I'm so far away from being a powerful female alpha it's laughable. I'm not going to need more mates."

Deacon opened his mouth then snapped it shut, and Cyrus looked at me like I was being stupid.

I turned to Knox, but even he was giving me a strange look.

"You resisted the full force of Cyrus's power and almost had him submitting to you," Knox said.

"That was your power," I told Knox. "I was channeling it through our bond."

Knox shook his head and my heart stuttered.

It hadn't been his power?

It had been *my* power?

That ferocious wildness that had roared through me was mine? It wasn't just a dream?

Impossible.

A hysterical laugh escaped my lips and I shook my head. I was weak. I'd always be weak. If I was an alpha, why hadn't my wolf woken? Why was I still... me?

"Your power might only be able to break through your curse when your mates are in danger," Cyrus said. "But that doesn't mean you won't have the side effects of being powerful. For all we know, unlike alpha females from this realm, you'll claim the mates you need like you claimed Knox and Bishop." His gaze jumped to Knox.

"Bishop will understand, but you need your wolf to be okay with that."

"Whatever protects Audrey," Knox growled, his eyes darkening with his wolf.

"So you'd just be fine with me being with other men?"

"If they're worthy, yes," he replied.

I wasn't going to ask what made someone worthy in Knox's eyes. It was all too much. Knox was agreeing to share me with someone, maybe multiple someones, even though I could feel his possessiveness toward me. And somehow, beyond my wildest dreams, I was an alpha. Except I could only reach my power when I was freaking out and even then, I had no control over it.

I hugged myself and curled into Knox's embrace. I really wanted Bishop. He'd know what to say to make sense of everything.

Was Cyrus right? Would I just claim whoever I needed whether I knew them or not? I didn't want to be mate bonded with a stranger again. Would fate be so cruel a second time or should I trust it? Things had worked out with Knox and I knew in my soul that he was mine, just like Bishop was mine.

I let my gaze wander to Cyrus who turned his attention to rotating our dinner on the spit.

My soul said he was mine, too, but I hadn't bonded with him.

I probably wasn't ready... or Cyrus wasn't. He'd made it clear he wasn't interested in me. Would that change?

And was there any point in worrying about it?

Fate was going to do what fate was going to do. Right now the only thing I did have control over was saving Bishop, and I damn well was going to do that.

AUDREY

I woke early the next morning, bleary-eyed after a restless sleep, my body aching from walking for two days straight and my core throbbing with need. Bishop's pain shot through me like agonizing zaps from an electric fence, more powerful and persistent than last night, despite the six elixirs we'd given him.

Only two more days.

We'd be at the pool in two days and then I'd have Bishop back.

"We're closer than that," Knox said, reading my thoughts with his telepathy as I eased out from between him and Bishop.

Except the moment I was no longer in contact with Bishop, his pain surged, stealing my breath and making my knees buckle.

His muscles contracted and a strangled moan escaped his lips, the precursor to a convulsion.

"Shit," Knox snarled, cushioning Bishop's head. "We just gave him an elixir two hours ago."

Whil scrambled for her pack and pulled out the small vial containing the only thing keeping Bishop alive, and I sagged back to the ground and pressed my hands against his cheeks. Instantly some of the tension released from his body, giving Whil enough time to pour the elixir down his throat.

Whil sat back on her heels and turned to Cyrus. "This is progressing faster than I expected."

"Then it's a good thing we're only a day away," Deacon said.

"But only if we leave now, push our pace, and keep walking after sunset," Cyrus replied, grabbing four ration bars from his pack and tossing them at me and Whil. "No time for breakfast."

I expected Deacon to make a joke about me walking and eating at the same time, but his expression remained serious which meant if I hadn't known it already, the situation was bad. Deacon always looked like he was trying not to spill an inside joke. And while he hadn't been as chatty as he'd been when I'd had dinner with him and Nova back in the Residence, he'd made an effort to keep us — probably just me — from having a complete breakdown.

Now he wasn't even trying.

I shoved my blanket into my pack and tried to stay in control of my emotions while Knox's were crashing through me.

It wasn't even two days now.

Sometime tonight we'd save Bishop.

If he lasted that long... and if Whil could actually pull out the poison.

She'd been confident when we'd left Stonehaven, but the veins in Bishop's flesh were thicker now and some of the larger veins had started weeping thick, black pus.

Bishop's pain surged again, making me stumble, but thankfully he didn't break out into a full convulsion. He trembled and moaned in Knox's arms, the few visible patches of skin left on his face gray, and sweat slicked his forehead.

God, was this the best the elixir could do for him now?

My once vibrant and powerful mate was weak and barely alive, and my heart broke just looking at him.

And there wasn't a damn thing I could do.

Even if I was as powerful as Cyrus, Knox, and Deacon seemed to think and I could actually access my alpha power, I still wouldn't be able to save him. Alpha power didn't work that way and neither did our soul bond. Unlike angelic mating bonds, shifters couldn't share life forces.

I was just as useless as I'd always been.

But that wasn't true. Just touching Bishop had helped ease his pain. Between Knox and I, we might have been slowing the progression of the poison with our souls' connections.

Another burst of pain made me stumble and Cyrus huffed.

"You seemed so confident yesterday that you could eat and walk," he said, scooping me into his arms.

I sighed. "Bishop's pain wasn't as bad yesterday."

"You can feel it?" He glanced at me, his expression a mix of pain and concern.

"You don't have to carry me," I said, dragging my attention to the forest in front of us before I fell into his moss green eyes and that stupid voice said he was mine.

"If we're going to make it to the pool tonight, I do."

"I could carry you," Deacon offered, a hint of mischievous mirth crinkling around his eyes.

"Fuck off, Deacon," Cyrus snarled, his voice dropping an octave into a sexy ramble and sending a shiver of need rushing down my spine and heating my core.

His nostrils flared at my arousal and my cheeks heated.

Stupid incomplete mating bond.

And stupid magical sex fairies. Now I knew what it felt like to be with Cyrus, to have his powerful arms hold me while his thick cock plunged into me again and again and again.

"Whatever you're thinking," Cyrus growled, "you need to stop."

Right. Because last night hadn't meant anything and he didn't want to be my mate... he just wasn't going to let Deacon carry me or me walk on my own.

"Then put me down."

"Finish your breakfast and I will." But his grip tightened as he spoke.

Was he lying? Had last night meant something?

Now I was just imagining things. We didn't even have a friendship. A relationship was pure fantasy.

Some of the sex glitter had to still be in my system. It was the only explanation for such a ridiculous thought, and I was only thinking it because I desired him and he'd brought up the multiple mates thing. My stress was through the roof and once again it was just us and a few others in the middle of nowhere.

I was confusing Cyrus's gruff kindness and practical suggestion for more than it really was. Everything would return to normal once we got back to Stonehaven and he had to become the pack alpha again.

If he really was mine, he was going to have to make his intentions clear. I'd drive myself crazy trying to figure out any subtle meaning behind his words and actions and expressions when they all said different things at the same time.

Except could I ignore that voice inside me?

Yes. Yes, I could.

If I didn't, it was only going to hurt.

Cyrus carried me for most of the morning and I'd never been so grateful to be distracted by the feel of his arms and his solid chest against my side or the barely-there warmth around my heart from our shifter connection. All of it managed to help me ignore Bishop's pain and Knox's emotions enough to stay more or less focused on my surroundings.

When the sun was high in the sky, he set me down, and I managed a few steps across relatively flat terrain before Bishop convulsed and the pain dropped me to my knees.

"Fuck," Cyrus snarled, grabbing me again and pressing me against Bishop to ease the convulsion so Whil could give him an elixir.

After that, he only set me down long enough for bathroom breaks. And as much as I wanted to do it on my own, I knew I wouldn't have been able to keep up even without Bishop's pain. The pace the guys set was just shy of a jog, and even Whil, with her magic enhancing her body, was barely keeping up.

Almost there, Knox said in my head as the sky started to turn dark gold with the beginnings of the sunset.

His emotions were hard, desperate, and icy as if he were trying to freeze our bond like he had when it had first formed. But this time it wasn't to keep me out. It was to protect me.

He grunted, and I glanced over Cyrus's shoulder at him as he caught his balance while Bishop thrashed in his arms.

We'd just given him an elixir less than an hour ago, but from the look of it — and the feel of his pain — he was going to need another one.

"How many elixirs do we have left?" I asked Whil.

"Two after this one," she said between gasping breaths.

"We have four hours to the pool," Deacon added. "We're not going to make it."

"Then we move faster." Cyrus stopped and turned so I could touch Bishop. "Whil, give him another. Deacon, take Whil. We're upping our pace."

A spike of fear surged through my bond with Knox.

"Can you handle that?" I asked him.

"Yes," he grunted as his fear grew stronger. His arms had to be tired. Even with his shifter strength, he couldn't keep carrying Bishop, especially with his constant small convulsions.

Knox's eyes narrowed and determination swept through the fear.

"Let's get moving," Cyrus snapped as Whil gave Bishop another dose of elixir.

Deacon swept her into his arms before she'd finished securing the clasp on her pack and started jogging.

Cyrus and Knox matched his pace. They ran until just after the sun sank below the horizon and a flickering light amongst the tree trunks ahead of us grew bright enough for us to make out a clearing with a person-sized statue of a woman pouring water from a large jug.

"Thank the Sisters," Knox groaned, relief cutting into his raging emotions.

We'd reached the pool with no time to spare. Thank God.

AUDREY

THE CLEARING WASN'T BIG, JUST WIDE ENOUGH FOR A couple of carts, and it was sheltered on two sides by naturally towering rock walls. The ground had been leveled and paved with flagstones and those flagstones narrowed along the far rock wall into a road that quickly turned into uneven ground with wheel ruts that led through the trees and off into the darkness.

"Alpha," a woman said as she stepped out of the shadows made by a recess in the closest rock wall.

She was a moderately powerful shifter radiating more than the regular level of feralness like Knox and Deacon and carried herself as if she were ready for a fight. But I didn't get the impression she was going to fight us, just that she was alert and prepared for danger.

"Alphas," she corrected herself. "What are you—" Then her gaze dipped to me in Cyrus's arms before sliding over the rest of the group.

"Thora, where's your Laisian partner?" Cyrus demanded as he set me down on shaky legs.

"Lewis is inside taking a piss." Thora jerked her thumb over her shoulder, making me realize the recess was actually the mouth of a cave with a wooden wall — complete with door — blocking it off.

As if speaking of him made him appear, the door opened and a middle-aged human warrior — wearing a leather jacket covered with metal rings — stepped out. His eyes widened when he saw us just as pain shot through my bond with Bishop and he released a strangled groan.

My knees buckled and Cyrus grabbed my arm and held me upright.

"We're using the pool," Cyrus growled, his alpha power pouring off him, making Thora gasp, but not affecting Lewis because he was human.

But Lewis didn't question or hesitate. He also didn't look scared about having to defend the pool against a powerful shifter. He just stepped aside and opened the door wider, allowing a soft band of warm light to spill across the flagstones.

"Don't worry," Deacon said as he strode inside. "We won't tell your king you just let us in."

"I don't really care if you do. Your hunters have kept us humans alive out here and he—" he pointed at Bishop, writhing in Knox's arms. "He doesn't look good."

"Thank you," Cyrus replied, heading toward the door with me in tow.

But a wave of panic crushed over me, stealing my breath and making me jerk away from him and cling to the doorframe.

Knox stood a few feet away, staring at the entrance, his breath suddenly too fast and his jaw clenched tight.

"I can take Bishop," Cyrus said as Whil stepped past us.

Pain tightened Knox's expression and frustration blended with his fear. "I can't let go."

My throat tightened, my heart breaking for him. He was so angry and afraid and now not just because Bishop was dying.

The only way to save Bishop was to take him inside, and we both knew the second Knox stopped holding him, he'd start convulsing, and we were out of elixirs.

"Knox," I said, shuffling the few feet to him and pressing my hands against his forearms to establish a physical connection.

He released a ragged breath and a hint of peace whispered through his emotions.

"You can do this." I shoved up my sleeves, adding more flesh to flesh contact while I fought to steady myself.

Somehow, I had to find the strength to reassure Knox, despite my own fears, and steady his soul so he could get Bishop to the pool.

But Bishop's pain was a constant burning in my limbs, Knox's emotions battered me from the inside, and I couldn't push past my own writhing emotions to focus. It was all a vortex pulling me under, suffocating and crushing me. It hadn't been as powerful this morning, but then Bishop's condition was quickly deteriorating.

I sucked in a ragged breath and squeezed my eyes shut, but that only made me more aware of everything raging inside me.

Damn it. Focus.

We were running out of time.

"Knox," I ground out, meeting his gaze.

Darkness filled his eyes, making the green specks stand out in sharp contrast, and I let myself fall into them. He was my ferocious mate, my strength and my protector, and I needed him now more than ever.

No. I *needed* his wolf. I needed to reach that primal part of his soul to push past his fear and do what needed to be done. Because if Bishop died, I'd lose both of them, and I didn't think I'd be able to survive that.

"Protect me." My pulse *thu-thudded*, hard and jarring, and jerked my whirling thoughts into focus. Nothing mattered except saving my mates and to do that I needed to steady Knox's soul.

Knox's eyes went completely black and his canines extended, his wolf taking over as I shoved love and certainty through our bond, steadying his soul.

He rumbled low in his throat, his power rolling off him, not in a demand of submission but in support, and I moved to his side and pushed my hands up under the back of his shirt to maintain contact.

Together, we marched through the door.

Inside, lit by magical glowing stones was a thirty by thirty room, half of it a living room with old, worn furniture, a fireplace, and a kitchenette, and the other half a storage area with stacks of wooden crates. It wasn't at all what I expected and there wasn't a pool in sight.

A door by the kitchenette stood partially open, revealing a toilet and sink, while another lay directly ahead of us. Deacon had his hand on the handle of that door, watching us enter, his expression tight.

"How long can you last?" he asked Knox as he opened the door, letting a wave of warm wet air wash over us and giving me a glimpse of the top of a large cavern with stalactites but not much else.

"As long as my mate needs me," his wolf growled back.

"Good," Cyrus said.

Beyond the door was a rock landing about ten feet off the ground and a shallow ramp that led down to the cavern floor. A shallow pool, the water glowing a soft blue, lay at the bottom of the ramp, and beside it was a deeper one.

Whil led us down the ramp and along a narrow, slippery path to the slightly deeper pool, set her pack on a ledge, and pulled out a thin, leather-bound book.

"We need to strip him and get him into the pool," she said, wiping sweat from her forehead. "You too, Knox and Audrey. You'll be able to get more flesh to flesh contact that way and I'm not taking any chances with this. I want your soul bonds steadying him."

"Right." I nodded, focusing on what needed to be done... because if I thought about stripping in front of everyone, I was going to panic, and I couldn't afford to panic. Not with Knox's tenuous grip on his claustrophobia.

Besides, getting naked in front of others was a natural shifter thing to do. Really.

And maybe if I kept telling myself that, I'd believe that I actually was a shifter and would stop being embarrassed about someone seeing me naked.

I could do this.

Just power through.

I pulled off my clothes as fast as possible and hopped into the water without making eye contact with anyone, especially Cyrus — even though he'd already seen me naked and I hadn't cared before.

The water was warm, verging on too hot, and the edge of the pool quickly sloped into the deeper water so I only needed a few steps before it was up to my shoulders.

Cyrus and Knox quickly stripped Bishop and, with Cyrus holding his head out of the water, they submerged him in the glowing liquid.

He groaned, his muscles contracting and releasing again and again with wave after wave of agony. The red and black veins pulsed like a too-fast heartbeat, churning my stomach, and the black pus oozing from the veins billowed around him, clouding the clear, shimmering water.

Please let this work, I prayed. *Please God or the Sisters or whatever gods or goddesses can hear me.* I needed him alive and well. I needed to tell him how much I loved him.

I pressed my body against his side and clung to his arm to avoid getting bashed in the face. Knox hopped in a second later and took over holding Bishop's head while also pressing himself against Bishop's side, pinning him between us.

A shuddering breath escaped Bishop's lips and the muscle contractions slowed down but didn't stop.

Whil knelt on the rock above his head, not stripping or getting in the water, and opened her book. "Whatever happens, just keep as much of him in the water as you can."

That didn't sound good.

KNOX

I clung to Bishop, wishing I was also in physical contact with Audrey because my insides were squeezed so tight I could barely breathe.

The cavern was bigger than the ballroom in the Residence where I could have spent an hour with only four other people in it, but it could have been as big as the arena and it still would have been too small right now. There weren't any windows and the only way out was the door where we'd entered and that led to an even smaller, windowless room.

My soul hadn't been steady since Bishop had been poisoned, and the only reason I hadn't shifted into my wolf and raced outside was because my brother and my mate needed me.

It was actually a miracle I was even in the cavern, but my smart mate had known exactly what I needed to fight through the fear threatening to crush me into nothing.

She'd called on my wolf's need to protect her. He would go through anything, *do* anything whether I wanted to do it or not to keep her safe, even if that took us to the edge of losing our humanity. And we were barely holding on.

"Make it quick," I growled at Whil as my wolf surged even stronger and pushed me farther back into my consciousness which also pushed back the primal feralness that would completely take over if he released even a fraction of his hold on me.

"That's the idea," Whil replied, scanning the book's pages.

Bishop groaned, his already twitching muscles contracting tight, arching his back, and pushing his chest out of the water.

More of the horrific black and red veins burst, oozing thick, viscous pus that clouded the pristine water, making me grit my teeth. All I could do was hold him. I hated that was all I could do while everything else was up to Whil.

"Come on, Bishop," Audrey murmured, pressing her forehead to his. "Just a little longer. Please." Her voice cracked, making both me and my wolf furious.

She shouldn't have to go through anything like this. Not now. Not ever. Yes, she'd proven she was strong — in her quiet, persistent, always-gets-back-up way — but if my wolf and I had anything to say about it, she'd never have to endure heartache and fear like this again.

It didn't matter that she had a powerful alpha locked

inside her. Even if she finally broke her curse, I wouldn't allow her to suffer.

"Okay." Whil handed Deacon the book, knelt by Bishop's head, and placed her hands on his forehead while Cyrus crouched beside her.

"If things go wrong," he said, glancing at Deacon, "you grab Whil. I've got Audrey."

Whil gave him a tight nod, her perpetual golden glow growing brighter as she focused on gathering her magic.

Blue light flickered in the water around us in response, cutting through the growing cloud of black pus. Then she closed her eyes, whispered a prayer to Ninti whose power imbued this water with magic, and light burst from her hands.

Bishop's head jerked back, threatening my grip, and a desperate howl of agony tore from his throat and ripped through our twin bond.

"Oh, God," Audrey gasped, her face suddenly white, her expression tight with Bishop's pain.

For a second, he was trapped in that horrible scream, his body locked in agony, then the pain flared stronger, whitening out my vision, and he thrashed with the full strength of an alpha shifter.

"Hold him still," Whil cried.

I tightened my grip and blinked my vision clear just in time to see Bishop slam his elbow into Audrey's face.

Her head snapped back and panic, stronger than Bishop's pain, shot through my bond with her. It vanished a second later and she went limp, unconscious.

"No," I lurched forward to rescue her.

"Stay!" Cyrus commanded with a blast of power, keeping me in place, and he grabbed Audrey's arm and hauled her head out of the water.

Blood poured from her nose, and I grabbed both of Bishop's arms and pinned them to his sides before he could accidentally hit her again. Thankfully, Deacon leaped in and secured Bishop's head so I didn't have to worry about drowning him.

"Come on, Audrey," Cyrus said, pushing Audrey's wet hair out of her face. "Your mates need you."

She groaned, her expression dazed for a moment before her eyes finally focused on Cyrus. Then realization, horror, and pain swept in before turning into determination.

She shoved out of Cyrus's arms and threw herself on Bishop as best she could with me in the way.

More blue light flashed through the water and Whil's breathing turned ragged. Sweat slicked her skin, soaked her shirt, and dripped into her eyes, but she kept her hands pressed against Bishop's forehead even as he bucked and twisted in my grip. The red and black veins pulsed, hard and fast and more of them burst, sending more black pus into the water.

Bishop screamed and gasped for what felt like forever but was probably only a few seconds. Then his flailing started to slow and his breathing grew labored. But the veins still covered him and they weren't going away.

He was losing strength, losing the fight against the

poison. I could feel the exhaustion and agony in our bond weakening his body and soul.

He wasn't going to give up and stop fighting. I could feel that, too. But he wasn't going to be able to go on for much longer and break my mate's heart.

"Fight it," I snarled at him. "Don't you dare fucking die." I shoved him against the stone slope. "Fight it. Don't. You. Die."

He groaned and his eyelids fluttered as if they were finally going to open after five days of unconsciousness. But instead, he sucked in a shallow breath, gurgled it out, and stopped breathing.

"No," Audrey gasped. "No. Please."

"Whil," Cyrus barked.

"Almost there," she ground out.

"He isn't breathing!" Cyrus snapped. "He—"

Audrey lurched forward and pressed her lips against Bishop's with a final kiss that made me want to scream.

This wasn't happening. No way in hell would this be their last kiss.

Except instead of actually kissing him, she breathed into his mouth.

"Audrey," Cyrus said, his voice breaking on her name, his alpha-in-control mask gone and his affection for her clear in the pain in his eyes.

"We'll save him. We just have to keep him alive long enough." She pulled back and felt for a pulse. "Too slow. I need him on a flat surface."

"He has to say in the water," Whil gasped.

"Fine," Audrey said, her expression fierce with determination. "Knox, start CPR. I'll keep doing the breathing."

Deacon shot her a wild look. "What the hell is CPR?"

"You don't—?" Her eyes widened then narrowed. "Knox, I'm teaching you CPR. Move aside. Hands here." She clasped her hands together, one on top of the other, and placed them on his chest. "Lock your elbows and push hard and fast, like this. Fifteen times. You're pumping his heart for him. Now show me."

I repeated her movements fifteen times and she gave Bishop a breath.

Another fifteen.

Another breath.

The golden glow around Whil's hands flared, and blue sparks jumped out of the water and sank into Bishop's face. More blue light flared around us, the flickers snapping faster and faster and I pumped my brother's heart while Audrey gave him breath. Again and again. Fifteen. Breathe. Fifteen. Breathe.

More of the black and red veins burst, except this time they didn't stay or get bigger, they drained their horrible pus into the water, shrinking until they were ugly black and red bruises under his skin.

"Come on, Bishop," Audrey said over and over again like a prayer, tears streaming down her cheeks while blood still oozed from her broken nose. "Please. Please. Come on. Please"

"Almost there," Whil gasped, her body trembling, her glow faint and flickering. "Just a little more."

Bishop gasped and his eyes fluttered open then closed again.

"Oh, God," Audrey cried, cupping his face and looking desperately at his closed eyes. "Tell me he's okay. Tell me he'll live."

AUDREY

"Tell me, please," I begged, trying to will Bishop into consciousness. He had to live. The thought that this wouldn't work, that we'd hiked as fast as we could and still failed was soul-crushing. It was worse than walking all the way to the death god's temple and failing to break my bond with Knox.

Whil's glow flickered bright for a second then completely vanished, and she collapsed against Deacon who held Bishop's head above the water.

My pulse lurched. She was out of magic and Bishop still hadn't woken up.

"No," I insisted, "just a little more. Please, Whil."

We were so close. Most of the veins had already sunk under his skin, but I could still see the poison lying like dark, horrific bruises under his flesh. She needed to get rid of all of it, every last stain to ensure he was safe.

My throat tightened and more tears streamed down

my cheeks. If Bishop died, I didn't think I'd ever stop crying.

More blue light snapped through the water, dancing over Bishop, wrapping around his torso before sinking into him.

He gasped and pain lanced through our bond as streaks of blue raced to each poisoned bruise. His muscles contracted, but Knox held on tight, stopping Bishop from hitting me in the face again.

"Come on, Bishop," Knox growled. "Fight."

The blue light glowed brighter than the bruises and spread until his entire body glowed and I could barely look at him.

The pain from our bond sparked, little zaps that made me jolt, but they were getting weaker and weaker.

Finally, with a brilliant flare of blue that forced me to close my eyes, the pain vanished.

"What—?" Bishop groaned, the words making my heart lurch with hope.

A second later, I realized the agony that had been a constant presence from the moment I'd bonded with Bishop was gone. All that remained was my relief and Knox's.

My eyes flew open, locking with Bishop's gaze and I was falling, falling, falling into a sea of warmth and love flecked with brilliant green stars.

"Audrey," he breathed and a giant wave of love crashed into me.

I gasped, shocked that I could feel Bishop's emotions so strongly before we'd even sealed our mating bond.

Then Knox's relief and concern swelled, crushing inside me, swirling and churning with Bishop's, becoming a giant whirling vortex. I was exhausted and confused and relieved and worried and afraid and everything at once.

It was too much. So much more than what I'd been fighting before.

I'd thought Knox's emotions had been overwhelming, but this was a tsunami, inundating me from all sides. I couldn't figure out what emotions were mine and which were theirs, unable to push through the onslaught from my mates.

I clutched my head as if that would help me focus and differentiate where they ended and I began, but their worry slammed into me, tearing at what little hold I had on myself.

The worry exploded into fear and someone reached for me, but I jerked away. I couldn't let them touch me. Physical contact would only make it stronger.

I needed space. I needed to breathe. I needed all the emotions to stop before I lost myself completely.

"Audrey," Knox growled, his fear roaring through me.

I pushed away from the slope, farther into the pool.

Get away get away get away.

Please.

"What's wrong with her?" Cyrus demanded.

"She's panicking but I don't know why," Knox replied as I fought to breathe and keep my head above the water.

More fear roared through me. I was going to drown, emotionally and physically, if I didn't pull myself together.

But was that my emotion or Knox's or Bishop's?

I grasped onto the emotion and tried to concentrate on it but couldn't tell where it had come from. Desperate, I tried to connect with my bonds. Maybe if I found them, I'd be able to tell which emotions were theirs, but I couldn't find my bonds in the consuming vortex inside me.

My head dipped into the water, shattering my concentration, and the vortex whirled stronger.

No. Please.

I flailed, heaving myself up long enough to break the surface and suck in a quick breath, before dipping back under.

Nothing was working and now all I could feel was panic. It made me thrash even when a barely audible voice in the back of my head knew if I just stayed calm I could tread water.

But everything was happening so fast, crashing around me, crushing my insides, and—

Strong hands grabbed me, hauled me up, and pinned me to a wide muscular chest. Heat swelled around my heart, my shifter connection latching on to whoever held me.

Except it was more than just a fellow shifter. The

connection was strong and steady, drawing me out of the vortex of emotions for a second, long enough for me to find a spark of myself and cling to it. It was someone my soul aligned with as if he were a mate or family... except the connection wasn't from Bishop or Knox.

"Can't take you anywhere," Cyrus rumbled and he cupped the back of my head with his hand and pressed my face into the crook of his neck, soothing me with his scent. "I should have asked if you could swim before I let you jump into the pool."

"I can swim," I groaned, hyperaware that I was completely naked and not caring that I was or that he didn't want me the way my soul wanted him, the way our shifter connection said we belonged together.

He carried me back to the edge of the pool and lifted me out of the water, setting me on the edge before pulling away. Except the loss of our connection let the vortex of emotions crash over me, twice as strong as before.

"Bishop, Knox, you need to try to block your bonds," Whil said with a weak voice.

"I'm not blocking my bond," Knox snarled as he reached for me. "Never again."

But the second he touched me, his emotions roared stronger, sending me spinning into darkness.

I heaved out of his grip, my heart breaking at the hurt in his eyes. "I'm sorry. I just— It's so hard to concentrate."

Cyrus hopped out of the water and clutched me to his chest again as I squeezed my eyes shut, sucking in ragged breaths and concentrating on the warmth around my heart from my shifter connection with him.

"I'm not letting you hold her all night," Knox spat. "She's my mate."

"And right now, you're overwhelming her with your bond," Whil said.

Knox growled. "I wasn't before. Not like this."

"She didn't have two mating bonds before," Whil huffed back. "You don't have to block it permanently, just until she can regain her bearings, and then you can carefully open it again. With both you and Bishop completely open to her, you're flooding her with emotions. Audrey —" Small hands grasped mine and I cracked open one eye to look at Whil.

She looked exhausted, her complexion was gray, and all of her golden glow was gone.

"Once you find your center, restrict the flow of their emotions. Just enough so they stop overwhelming you."

I nodded and leaned into Cyrus, needing all the steadiness I could get from his soul.

Slowly, the roar of emotions from Knox and Bishop eased, getting quieter and quieter until I could recognize my soul bonds with them and which emotions were theirs.

The heat around my heart grew and so did a warmth in my core. I was completely naked in Cyrus's powerful arms, my body pressed against his naked, muscular chest, and my soul ached for him to recognize that we were meant to be together.

Which was not what I was supposed to be thinking about.

I dragged my attention away from him and concentrated on turning down the volume on both Knox's and Bishop's emotions.

"That's it, beautiful," Bishop murmured.

He stared at me, his love and desire surging through our incomplete bond, not overwhelming me like before, but igniting a suddenly wild, primal desire within me.

The sensation exploded through my body, searing my nerves, turning them instantly hypersensitive, and making my breasts and core ache. My breathing turned ragged, and I trembled in Cyrus's grip, desire leaking from my core, my body instantly ready for what it wanted.

BISHOP

Need for Audrey tore through me, all consuming and wild. My cock went instantly hard and my wolf took over.

Mine. Audrey was mine.

I could feel it in my soul, in the incomplete mating bond wrapped around my heart. Somehow, even though it had only been a dream and neither of us had said the vows, Audrey had claimed me as hers. And completing the bond was the only thing I could think about.

I'd deal with what had happened, where the hell I was, and why it felt like I had cracked ribs later. Right now, I needed Audrey, needed to bury myself deep inside her and sink my teeth into her and complete the bond. And then, after she was fully mine, I needed to punch whoever had broken her nose.

"Wouldn't you rather someplace more comfortable?"

Whil asked, placing a hand on my shoulder, but I jerked away and snarled at her.

No one was taking me away from my mate.

"Come on, Whil," Deacon said, urging her away from me. "His wolf is in charge right now, and from Audrey's scent, she's practically in heat."

My mate's face turned red, adorably embarrassed that Deacon was talking about her body signaling me that she wanted to mate.

Except my human half knew I should take care of her and not claim her on the stone floor of... where was I? A cavern? The healing pool?

Mine. Now, my wolf snarled.

He'd wanted to claim her from the beginning and had patiently waited while I courted her. But no more. She'd almost died when that man— no, that *thing* had attacked her. It hadn't smelled like a shifter, a human, or any other race I was familiar with. My wolf wasn't going to wait a minute longer.

And while my wolf wasn't nearly as wild as Knox's, he was still a primal, ferocious predator.

I can't stay, Knox said in my head, his telepathic connection drawing my attention to our twin bond and his emotions.

He was relieved that I was safe, but also barely hanging on from going feral, the fear of being inside a vise around his chest.

I turned to him. His expression was tight, and I

grabbed the back of his head and pressed our foreheads together.

She's safe with me, I assured him.

I know, he replied. *I just want—*

What we had in the dream, I finished for him.

But your claiming should be just you two, he added, knowing my thoughts.

With a snarl, he jerked away from me. "Don't you dare leave her unsatisfied."

He stormed over to Audrey, still clutched tight in Cyrus's arms, and kissed her with a claiming ferocity that made the scent of her arousal spike and flood the air.

Then he jerked back, making her whimper, her lips chasing his, desperate for more.

"Next time," she breathed, watching him shift and race out of the cavern. Then her gaze jumped to me and her pupils dilated with lust.

"Mine," she growled, the sound low and dangerous, making my already hard cock harder.

Sisters! She was the sexiest woman I'd ever seen, and I liked this confident side of her, even if it was only her need riding her hard.

The tip of her tongue flicked out, wetting her lips, and she pulled out of Cyrus's embrace and crawled toward me.

A rumbling purr rattled in Cyrus's chest, there one second then gone so fast I might not have believed I'd heard it if his hungry gaze wasn't locked on her pussy. Her position put her on full display to him, but from her intent gaze on me, she had no idea what she was doing to him.

Sucking in a sharp breath, he shoved to his feet, as if he hadn't just reacted to her, and pretended the massive tent in his soaked pants wasn't giving him away.

He wanted our mate.

How long was he going to use the excuse of pack responsibilities to ignore what was obvious — or at least obvious to me?

I could see him being a complete idiot and trying to ignore it for the rest of his life... although maybe not.

When I'd regained consciousness, he'd been holding her as if they belonged together. There hadn't been any hint of him holding himself back and overthinking the situation like he usually did with women he was attracted to. He'd been acting on instinct, which told me his wolf had already decided. Audrey was his mate.

Hopefully, it was just a matter of time before his human half accepted the truth.

"We'll be outside," he said, his voice gruff as he pulled out a shirt and pants from a travel pack and set them beside a pile of smaller clothing haphazardly thrown on the ground near the cavern wall. "Come on."

He stormed in the same direction Knox had fled with Deacon and Whil close at his heels, leaving me and Audrey alone.

"Come here," I commanded, giving my wolf full control. Audrey and I had had our sweet bonding in our shared dream and now it was my wolf's turn.

A snap of my power broke free of my hold and compelled her to obey. But instead of being upset that I'd used my power on her, the hunger in her expression deepened. In fact, it didn't seem as if my power had affected her—

No, that wasn't right. It *had* affected her, but it hadn't commanded her. Instead, it awakened a power within her, something that I'd thought had just been a part of our shared dream, and not something that could happen in reality.

It was radiant and strong, stronger than it had been in our dream, and it rolled over me, a hot wave challenging my power and bringing it to the surface as if I wasn't the one in control of it, shocking me.

My wolf rumbled with pleasure, sucking in deep breaths of her arousal, waiting for her to come to him. Then, when she was mere inches away, he pounced, ignoring the pain in our chest. He grabbed her and rolled until she was pinned against the slope in the pool with our body.

"Mine," we snarled and she tipped her head back, exposing her neck.

"Claim me, alpha," she moaned, her hips already rocking up, rubbing her heated core against my cock.

I took her lips in a ferocious kiss fueled by my wolf's need to mate her and she kissed back, just as needy. Our tongues battled and our teeth clicked. Her fingers dug into my shoulders, and she ground herself against me as if she'd been aching with need for too long and was desperate for a release.

It was beautiful torture, her body begging for me, the whisper of her lust teasing through the bond making my wolf crazy.

I roughly palmed her breast, kneading her soft flesh and drawing a moan of pleasure. Her nipple tightened and I dipped into the water to suck on it.

Her lust coming through our bond swelled, swirling with mine. My heart raced and my soul strained toward her desperate to complete what we'd started in our dream.

I needed her more than I needed to breathe. My soul was incomplete without her. It always had been, and I'd always known I was waiting for someone amazing, someone who saw my twin for who he really was, who'd accept both of us.

I thrust forward, grinding down and hitting her clit. Her hips twitched, the jerky movement rubbing just where she needed, making her shiver and moan but not taking her over the edge.

I could feel the tension building in her through our bond as well as her frustration.

"Bishop, please," she begged. "I need you in me. I need to seal our bond."

My wolf released a snap of power, and her body shook. A throaty moan escaped her lips and her breaths turned ragged. She teetered on the edge, aching with a need that sent tingles racing up my spine. Every fiber of her being strained for more, for me, for our bond to be completed.

With a snarl, my wolf drew back our hips, drawing a whimper of displeasure from our mate, then plunged inside her with one powerful stroke.

Her walls fluttered around our cock with a whisper of the orgasm I was going to give her, and she released a cry of pleasure.

"Yes," she moaned, her head tipping back and turning to the side to expose her neck. "Make me yours."

"You've always been mine," my wolf snarled. "Always been fated for me."

My canines extended as I pounded into her with wild, ferocious strokes. I overwhelmed her with pleasure, making her moan and gasp, and the feeling of her desire roared through me.

Mine. Always mine.

She clung to me and bucked her hips, meeting me stroke for stroke, our bodies crashing together in a primal dance, our souls entwining tighter and tighter. Her channel quivered, its grip straining my hold on my release. But she needed to come first, always first — and multiple times once our bond was sealed.

She moaned my name, repeating it over and over again like a prayer, and strained her neck, tilting it as far as it could go.

Then her muscles clamped down hard on me and she screamed her release. That threw me over the edge. With a final thrust, my cum erupted from me, filling her up, satisfying my wolf's need to mate, and I sank my teeth into her neck just above Knox's mating marks.

Sensation roared through our bond, bliss, satisfaction, joy, and love, so much love. It flooded my soul and radiated warmth across my chest. It sank deep into every fiber of my being and locked into place. We were finally connected the way we were supposed to be, the way it had always been meant to be.

"I love you," she murmured. Her words were slurred, and I could feel her exhaustion rushing in.

"I love you, too," I whispered back as she passed out. "Always."

AUDREY

I woke in Bishop's arms, lying on a futon and covered with a light, soft blanket. We were in a small room with exposed thick stone blocks along the back wall and small blocks making up the other walls. Sunlight poured through a narrow window above our heads, and at our feet stood a plain wooden door. My whole face throbbed and I could barely open my right eye, but I'd happily pay the price of a broken nose again to ensure Bishop survived.

"There you are," he rumbled, the sound vibrating in my chest and setting off a soft, delicious warmth between my thighs. It wasn't a desperate need like it had been before and it certainly wasn't anywhere near the level of my heat. It was just me reacting to being naked in the arms of a sexy naked man who loved me.

"I could feel you waking up through the bond but it took you a minute to open your eyes," he said, pressing his lips against the top of my head and squeezing me tighter. "That's going to take some getting used to. I'm not even that connected with Knox and our twin bond is unusually strong."

"It is weird and there are some downsides to being able to sense each other's emotions," I told him. "We can't keep anything from each other, even if it's a lie to spare my feelings."

"Not much of a downside if it means I'll know when you need me and what you need."

I snuggled in closer, breathing in his bright, fresh-cut grass scent. He was alive and safe and mine, and I could feel through our bond that he was thrilled to be my mate. His love shimmered bright and warm around my heart and, just like I felt with Knox, I felt like I was home with Bishop.

Of course, I'd always felt like I belonged with Bishop. Not once had he made me feel unwanted or weak or unworthy. Everything Bishop had done had been to build me up, to prove I deserved love, and that there wasn't anything wrong with me, even though I couldn't shift.

But I also knew, if I'd bonded with him first, I'd never have bonded with Knox, and my soul needed Knox as much as it needed Bishop. I wasn't sure how I knew that or if I really was as powerful as they said and that was the reason I needed both of them — and Cyrus, too, if I was being honest with myself — but I felt more settled and at peace with who and where I was than I'd ever been before.

Bishop stroked a gentle hand along my cheek, his fingers skimming too close to my broken nose, spiking pain through my throbbing face and making me wince.

"Sorry." He jerked his hand away and leaned back so he could look me in the eyes. "Cyrus said I'm the one who hurt you."

Shame flickered through our bond and I responded by sending him more love.

His eyes widened in surprise. "*That's* going to take some getting used to, too. Can I do that?"

The shame vanished, replaced by curiosity. Then a massive wave of love and desire flooded me, making my heated core ache with need.

"Oh!" he gasped, then his voice lowered and his pupils dilated with desire. "I see. I've left my mate wanting."

With a sexy groan, he captured my lips in a long, sweltering kiss that stole my breath and left me gasping. His desire spun around and wove through mine with a heady rush of emotions that both of us could feel, drawing another sexy groan from him.

"You mentioned the disadvantage of the bond," he purred, teasing his lips down my neck and flicking his tongue against his mating mark.

Sensation jolted through me, rushing straight to my core and making me moan.

"But you didn't mention the advantages," he added.

He teased his lips to my breasts and sucked on one

nipple then the other, working them into tight buds, before pushing the blanket aside and moving lower.

His need and love and awe roared through me before shifting into a ferocious hunger. He settled between my thighs and buried his nose in my curls, breathing in my scent.

Tremors of anticipation fluttered through my core, and he hummed in satisfaction, now knowing — because of our bond — how much I wanted him.

"Bishop," I moaned, tangling my fingers in his hair. "Don't make me wait."

"As my mate commands."

He swept his tongue through my folds in a slow, sensual stroke, sending shivers rushing up my spine. I moaned again and sank into the sensation. His desire and mine swirled together and grew stronger as he worked me to the edge.

I clung to him, riding the building wave, my hips bucking into his mouth. He pushed a finger inside me and sucked on my clit, drawing me closer and closer.

Right to the edge.

Then he pulled back before I could come, making me whimper in disappointment.

"I've got you, Audrey," he said, crawling up my body and kissing me, filling my mouth with the flavor of my desire.

The head of his cocked pushed at my opening and slowly — so damned slowly — he pushed inside me. My breath picked up, my pulse racing with anticipation while he bottomed out then held still, fighting to control himself.

"You feel so good and with our bond, it's even more intense." He met my gaze, capturing me with his warm brown eyes and the mesmerizing bright green flecks. "So perfect."

His love flooded me and he began to move, his pace getting faster and faster and my desire spinning tighter and tighter, taking me higher than he had before, and sending me spiraling over the edge.

My satisfaction sent him over the edge as well and together we whirled in bliss, his and mine mingling, feeding each other, before slowly releasing us.

A moment later someone knocked on the door.

"Well that sounded satisfying," Deacon chuckled through the door, making my face burn with embarrassment. "Wish I could give you more time, but our mighty leader wants to head out."

"Tell him Audrey needs to rest," Bishop replied.

Deacon snorted. "That didn't sound like resting."

"We've just bonded," Bishop insisted. "You know we're not going to be able to keep our hands off each other."

"You couldn't keep your hands off her before," he laughed. "But if you want more time, then you'll have to tell him yourself."

Bishop tipped his head back and groaned. "How long did it take us to get here?"

"Five days, and yes, Cyrus plans a slower pace so six or seven days back," Deacon replied.

"And the alliance meeting in Stonehaven will only be a few days after that," Bishop groaned. "That doesn't give us much time to prepare."

"Exactly. The bathrooms are at the end of the hall to your right, the stairs to the first floor beside them," Deacon said. "You probably have enough time to clean up and eat breakfast before Cyrus starts getting agitated. Oh, and watch your nudity. There are humans around."

Bishop sighed. "Looks like we should get up."

"If we don't, the next person at our door will be Cyrus, and I doubt he'll knock," I replied.

A small shiver of desire rushed down my spine at that thought but thankfully Bishop didn't comment on it. The bond didn't tell us where the other person's emotions were coming from, although sometimes it was pretty easy to guess.

Someone had brought our packs to the small room, leaving them in a neat row by the door, and Bishop grabbed a pair of pants while I wrapped myself in the blanket — not wanting to put on clean clothes until I'd bathed.

It wasn't a walk of shame if you were doing it with your mate.

"Sisters, you're so beautiful," Bishop groaned, his gaze raking down my body. "When we get back—"

"You'll have the meeting with the alliance members to prepare for." And I had no doubt Bishop was necessary.

Cyrus could conduct business and negotiate the best deal for the pack, but he needed Bishop's social finesse to put the alliance members at ease.

"There'll be times when I can get away. And besides —" He wiggled his eyebrows at me. "You do have another mate to keep you satisfied." He grabbed our packs before opening the door, gesturing for me to step out into a narrow, windowless hall lit by glowing stones. "Then after the meeting, you're all mine for at least a week."

"Just a week?" I asked with a chuckle, turning right and heading to the bathroom while pretending not to see the three men at the end of the hall staring at us. "Pretty sure we're mated for life."

"The week is just for us," he said, leaning close and dropping his voice to that sexy low rumble that always turned me on. "After that, I'll share you with my brother."

Heat blossomed across my cheeks and in my core, making both of us groan.

One of the men at the end of the hall gave us a knowing look before ushering the other two — who looked surprised — down the stairs.

"Damn," he said, clutching his chest in mock agony. "Teasing you now teases me. That's not fair."

I laughed at him. "I'd say that's only fair."

"Nothing is fair with you, beautiful. You can slay me with a smile and I'll always die happy."

"Yeah, well," I said, trying to get my blush under control. "Hold off on the dying for... I don't know... close to a century or so."

His expression softened and he pulled me into a warm embrace. "I promise. No dying. I'll never leave you, Audrey."

"I know." My throat tightened with all the fear I'd been fighting since he'd been poisoned.

"You'll never be alone again," he murmured as he pressed his lips to my forehead. Then he released a soft huff. "But we now have to change the conversation. Knox just yelled at me for making you upset."

I squeezed Bishop tighter, savoring his fresh green scent, and sent love to Knox to reassure him that I was fine.

This was going to be a very strange relationship, but I wouldn't change it for anything. I was with the people I was supposed to be with and loved by two incredible men.

AUDREY

Bishop and I separated and went into the appropriate bathrooms — Bishop having to point out which door said woman. Inside the women's bathroom was a long counter with three sinks and a wide mirror reflecting just how bad I looked.

My hair was a mess, my skin too pale from barely getting any sleep and overexerting myself, and my face was a swollen, bruised mess.

Thankfully, it didn't look like my nose was completely out of shape, so at least when it healed, I'd look more or less normal, but both of my eyes had blackened.

I couldn't believe Bishop had made love to me while I looked like a raccoon or called me beautiful. But I guess that was what it meant to be in love. I'd make love to Bishop no matter what he looked like because he was mine and we were meant to be together.

Across from the counter were three toilet stalls and

tucked around a corner was an area with a bench, another counter, and three wide shower stalls. At the far end of the counter was a rack with fluffy towels and a half-full bin with used towels.

I quickly cleaned up, got dressed — ignoring my reflection in the mirror — and returned to the hall where Bishop was waiting for me. We took the stairs down one flight to the first floor and stepped into a cafeteria.

The room wasn't big with half a dozen long tables and benches, but it looked warm and inviting. The whole left side was filled with tall, wide windows letting in streams of sunlight and looking out onto a square with grass and flowerbeds and benches.

A cluster of tall trees shaded half the square and with the rocky ground rising up in front and to the right, it gave the square a feeling of peaceful seclusion. A couple sat on one of the benches chatting while another woman was weeding one of the flower beds.

Inside, opposite the windows was an open kitchen where a stout, older man stood at the stove cooking something that smelled amazing, and at the far end sat the three men who'd been watching us.

"Morning, alpha," the cook said. "I'm just cooking up some extra sausage for you because I know how much meat you wolves like to eat." He winked at us and rolled half a dozen large sausages onto a platter then set it on the counter behind me. "There's also fruit and pancakes."

"Thank you," Bishop replied with a huge smile. "Everything smells incredible."

I took half a sausage, a couple of pancakes, and an orange — something I hadn't seen a lot of in Stonehaven — and we sat at one of the tables and ate. A few minutes later, Cyrus, Deacon, and Whil joined us.

"Sisters," Deacon breathed, looking at my face. "It didn't look that bad last night."

"It can take a while for bruises to form," Whil replied. "Here." She handed me a large cup filled with water. "Drink this."

Blue light flickered in its depths reminding me of the healing pool last night, and I raised my eyes in question. She'd pulled the poison out of Bishop and released it in the pool, not to mention none of us had cleaned up before we'd hopped in and Bishop and I— Well, I was pretty sure we defiled it by completing our mating bond.

"The pool purifies itself and it was clean when we woke this morning. All trace of poison and anything else was gone," she said. "This isn't as refined as an elixir, which is why you have to drink so much, but it should help with your nose."

"Hopefully, you won't look like you lost a fight by the time we get back to Stonehaven," Cyrus said, his voice gruff.

"Hopefully," I repeated. I hadn't thought about what returning to Stonehaven would be like, especially if it looked like I'd been beaten up.

I was now mated to two of the pack's alphas, and while it was obvious I was weak, I didn't want it to be painted on my face. Who knew what I'd be up against when we returned. Velora and anyone else who had their heart set on being Bishop's mate would be furious with me, not to mention I'd been with Bishop when he'd been poisoned. Those who didn't like me before were probably spreading rumors that I was somehow responsible.

Except, wasn't I?

That man had been trying to poison me, not Bishop, and had only run away because Bishop would have killed him before he could touch me.

And there wasn't anything I could do about that. I couldn't convince people to like me. I'd never been able to convince anyone of anything. I just had to be careful, stick with the people I could trust, and live my life.

I drank Whil's not-elixir and finished my breakfast while the others talked about our return trip. When we were done, we returned our dishes to the cook and thanked him again then headed out of the building — which was built flush against a tall rock wall — into the outside square, and around to a set of wide steps.

The steps were carved into the rock wall beside the building and led up to the courtyard I'd seen last night with the statue of the woman pouring water and the entrance to the sacred pool. Knox, in his wolf form, lay by the statue watching the stairs.

He bounded over to me the second he saw me, and I wrapped my arms around his neck and nuzzled my face in his soft fur, breathing in his rich, wood smoke scent. Relief and love rushed through our bond and I sent relief and love back to him.

Bishop joined us in the hug and warmth billowed around my heart, our shifter connection aligning our souls, comforting and assuring us: this was who we were supposed to be with.

I wanted to be with you, Knox said, his emotions indicating he'd wanted to be close not necessarily have sex. *But Bishop needed you more and you deserved to sleep on a bed.*

"Thank you," I told him. "I love you and I promise, I'll work on getting us that greenhouse bedroom."

"A greenhouse bedroom?" Bishop asked.

"Knox and I spent the entire night together in Whil's greenhouse, which means he can be inside, it just has to be a glass room," I replied.

She wants to build it on the Residence's roof, Knox replied with a chuckle.

"So no one can see us naked!"

"What's this about naked?" Deacon asked, laughing as my face turned red. He'd seen *everything* last night and I had a foggy memory of maybe flashing Cyrus my privates... but I wasn't a hundred percent sure on that. The need to complete my bond with Bishop was all that I really remembered after saving him.

"She wants to build a greenhouse bedroom for Knox so they can spend the night together," Bishop said.

Deacon's eyes flashed bright, but it wasn't with amusement. It was with surprise and happiness. "That's a brilliant idea."

"And something we'll deal with once we get back to

Stonehaven," Cyrus growled. "Let's get moving. I'm setting an easier pace but that doesn't mean we should waste time."

"Yes, alpha," Deacon chuckled, making Cyrus frown. "What? You *are* the alpha."

"But you only call me that when you're being a pain in my ass," he grumbled. "You and Nova."

Deacon's smile grew bigger. "It's our job. But you are right. Whil, can I carry your pack?"

"Absolutely," she replied, handing it over.

AUDREY

WE LEFT THE HEALING POOL AT A SLOWER PACE THAN WE arrived, for which I was grateful. I wasn't as sore as I'd been walking north, but I was still sore. Bishop held my hand while Knox, in his wolf form, kept brushing up against me, and my heart couldn't have been fuller.

On top of that, a gentle breeze whispered through the forest and the sun shone brightly, turning into brilliant specks of dancing light with the fluttering leaves and branches.

Even Cyrus looked more relaxed. He and Deacon chatted about the upcoming alliance meeting and their thoughts about the merchants with the weapons powerful enough to take down a grimalkin.

"If they do what Gower claims, this could change things," Deacon said.

"Yes, we'd suffer fewer casualties but we have to weigh how this will also affect our alliances, not to mention anyone who wants to hurt or conquer us," Cyrus replied.

"You know I hate it when you bring a good thing down," Deacon huffed.

"But you know he's right," Bishop replied. "If Gower buys enough of these weapons he won't need our warriors, and our warriors and Whil's elixir are our primary export."

"Not until Audrey works her magic with her new technology," Deacon said, flashing me a teasing smile.

Cyrus slowed his pace to fall into step with Bishop. "New technology?"

"I might not have anything soon," I replied, glaring at Deacon, who just kept smiling at me. I hadn't been sure if Deacon, Nova, Whil, or Bishop had mentioned to Cyrus my plan to tell the pack's scientists and engineers about stuff from my realm, but it was clear they hadn't. I'd been planning to keep it a secret and not draw attention to myself until I actually had something to show Cyrus. I wanted him to see I was valuable to the pack, and I couldn't do that without proof.

"What kind of timeline are we talking about?" Cyrus asked.

"I don't know."

He frowned at me, but instead of wanting to shrink away from him like I used to, I just felt frustrated. I hadn't even started working with anyone, and I was still learning what the pack knew and didn't know.

Sensing my frustration, both Knox and Bishop hit me

on both sides with a wave of confidence and determination. The emotions were so strong, I stumbled, needing to clutch Bishop's hand and lean against Knox to keep my balance.

Cyrus groaned and looked skyward. "We aren't even walking that fast."

Deacon's shoulders shook, and he clamped his jaw shut then slapped his hands over his mouth then gave up, releasing a deep laugh. The sound was contagious and soon all of us were laughing and I'd just couldn't stop.

It was like the final wall I'd put up to protect myself from the stress of trying to save Bishop had shattered, and all the worry and fear came rushing out in a laugh. The situation hadn't even been that funny.

"Really, though," Bishop said, sucking in deep breaths and trying to get himself under control. "That was our fault. You were frustrating her and we both sent support through our bond at the same time." He palmed the back of his neck and looked sheepish. "Next time, I won't be so forceful."

Me, too, Knox said.

"I don't mind," I assured them. I'd rather be knocked off my feet with love and support than anything else. That, and I liked how determined they were to show me that they had my back. No one else had ever been so certain. Not even Mila, who'd been my only friend in my old pack.

Sure, she cared for me but not enough to stand up against our alpha for me, and I wouldn't have expected that from her, either. She had a medium level of shifter strength but that still wasn't enough for Merrick to respect her. I wasn't sure if Merrick respected anyone.

Cyrus huffed and rolled his eyes. "I'm not criticizing or stopping you. I want to help and I need to know where you are in the process so I can provide the proper support."

Warmth fluttered around my heart at his words, a hint of a shifter connection forming even though we weren't touching. Or was that something else? The connection my soul was determined to make with him that I doubted he'd ever accept.

"I'm at the 'I don't know what I don't know' stage," I said, making him frown again.

"We've been spending time together," Whil added, "and I've been answering her questions about our realm and our pack."

"For example, lenses," Deacon said. "And I've talked to a few different human merchants and still don't know if they've figured out how to correct bad eyesight or not."

"What does human eyesight have to do with anything?" Cyrus asked.

"If they've figured out what concave and convex lenses do," I told him, "they'll have invented glasses to help people see better as well as magnifying glasses and telescopes."

A wrinkle formed between Cyrus's eyebrows. "I have no idea what those are. Those words sound weird."

"They sound weird to me, too," Deacon said and

everyone else nodded, even Whil who had more experience traveling beyond the pack's lands.

"I guess that means the magic that lets me understand and speak to you can't translate the words." Which suggested that for whatever reason, no one had discovered those things.

"So like *hors d'oeuvres*," Bishop piped in.

Cyrus threw his hands up and groaned. "What the hell is an *hors d'oeuvres*? A new technology as well?"

"It's a mini appetizer," I told him. "But the magic doesn't translate it because it's not my native language."

Deacon looked at me as if he'd never seen me before. "You speak more than one language in your realm?"

"No," Bishop said on my behalf, eager to share what he'd learned, but then looked at me, his expression — and his emotions from the bond — guilty for answering when he didn't actually know if I spoke more languages or not.

I smiled at him and shook my head, sending him encouragement through the bond so he'd keep going. We'd had the conversation days ago during a picnic lunch and he was still excited at the idea of me helping the pack with what I knew.

"They have ways of communicating long distances so some foreign words have become common use."

"That's incredible," Deacon replied. I'd mentioned the lenses during one of our dinners together when Bishop was away, but I hadn't talked about all the other things from my world.

"What would be the fastest and easiest thing to make?" Cyrus asked.

"The lenses," I replied without hesitation. I'd been thinking about what needed the least amount of learning since I'd started seriously learning about this realm. "They require creating perfectly clear glass which you already have on some of your windows and creating the glass with a curve... and I'm not sure the best way to go about doing that."

Cyrus pursed his lips, his gaze traveling into the woods ahead of us as he thought. "When we get back, I'll set you up with Isac. He's our best glassmaker. He should be able to make what you need."

His attention jumped back to me, his eyes bright with determination, something I'd never seen from him before. The look made my heart flutter and a sliver of the warmth in my chest slipped down to my core. That annoying voice inside me started to speak up, but I shove it aside, not wanting to shatter the moment.

Except he must have seen something in my eyes, because he grunted and looked away, shattering the moment.

"The faster you make something, anything," he said, his voice gruff. "The faster the reluctant members of our pack will accept you."

BISHOP

I couldn't stop looking at Audrey. Even with both her eyes bruised and her face slightly swollen, she was still the most beautiful woman I'd ever seen. She practically glowed with relief, and the sense I got through our mating bond was that everything was right... well, almost right. *Almost* right because of my surly, obstinate older brother.

But now I knew why he was holding back *and* that he'd realized a solution. He wasn't going to die thinking he had to mate with a woman the pack would accept. He just had to make the pack accept the woman he wanted.

We hiked until the sun reached the horizon, moving at an even slower pace than the one we'd set for Audrey after her heat, and I was still exhausted when Deacon found us a campsite.

We'd even stopped for a longer than normal lunch, Cyrus making sure Audrey had eaten everything before moving on — apparently there'd been something about walking and choking while I'd been unconscious, and Cyrus was his usual overprotective self — which I wasn't going to complain about.

Audrey was everything to me, and while I knew I shouldn't treat her like glass and she wasn't going to break, I couldn't calm my need to keep her safe.

Part of that came from Knox, his wolf riding him hard after all the stress from the last couple of days, but the other part was all me.

The poison that had nearly killed me with my more powerful healing had been meant for Audrey. And the *thing* that had attacked us hadn't smelled natural.

Cyrus ordered Knox to hunt, Deacon to gather firewood, and Whil to find berries and greens to supplement our dinner. Then he grabbed our canteens to fill them at the nearby river, leaving me alone with my mate since we'd woken up this morning.

"How are you feeling," Audrey asked me, gathering enough wood from the surrounding forest to start a fire.

"Tired," I confessed.

"You feel tired." She stacked the wood like I'd taught her and pulled a starter from her pack. "I remember when Cyrus asked me if I could start a fire without a starter as if everyone could do that."

"Most of us can," I replied. "We learn as pups, but the starter is faster and more consistent."

She rolled her eyes at me, a soft smile tugging at her lips and the feeling of a groan teasing through our bond

— and not the sexy kind of groan, the kind made when Deacon told a bad joke.

"I'd like to see him in my realm." She lit the kindling and gently breathed on the flames, encouraging them to grow. "Tell him to turn on a smartphone and make a call. We all learn *that* as children."

I snorted a laugh. "I have no doubt Cyrus would be lost in your realm, and I doubt he'd be as gracious learning all the things he'd need to know to survive as you were."

"Yeah, I could see a whole bunch of broken phones. God, I can't imagine him behind the wheel of a car. All the other drivers doing crazy driver stuff would drive him crazy."

I sighed, my chest aching with longing. "I really wish I could visit your realm, see you in your element."

Her gaze dropped to her hands, an action born of years of abuse that she probably wouldn't be able to completely get rid of.

"I wasn't that impressive there, either."

"You weren't given a chance to be impressive," Whil said as she stepped through the underbrush about twenty feet away. "And I wish I *could* open the gate, allow you and the boys the share each other's realms. I think I've figured out how to recreate the spell that brought you here, but..."

"But it involves an incomplete mating bond," Audrey replied as her expression darkened, probably remembering the horrible events that brought her to our realm.

"Yes and I'm not willing to do that to someone." Whil set her foraging down — a collection of wild spinach and mushrooms that would go well with whatever Knox caught — and started pulling the collapsible rotisserie and everything else we needed to make dinner out of our packs.

"You shouldn't," Audrey said, settling in my lap and cuddling against me.

Her scent flooded my senses, sweet and fresh, as warmth billowed around my heart and contentment radiated through our bond.

I wrapped my arms around her, drawing a soft sigh, while trying to ignore my hardening cock. She wouldn't want everyone watching, or even just hearing us have sex, and really, we were both too tired for it.

A few minutes later, Deacon returned with an armful of firewood, then Cyrus came back with our canteens. A few minutes after that, Knox returned with a perfectly skinned and gutted goat... in his human hands and not his wolf's teeth.

Deacon raised his eyebrows in surprise.

"What?" Knox huffed, handing him the goat.

Deacon continued to stare in disbelief as Knox stormed to my side, sat, and pulled Audrey into his lap.

A part of me wanted to protest that she was mine and our bond was still new, but the rest of me knew he needed this. He'd been under extreme stress and hadn't gone feral, but also hadn't been able to hold Audrey because he'd been holding me, keeping me alive.

"Audrey, you *are* a goddess," Deacon said in exaggerated awe, drawing a growl from Knox. "I've rarely seen him choose to be human."

"Don't poke him," Cyrus warned. "I won't stop him if he wants to pick a fight."

"I'm happy to help him let off steam," Deacon shot back. "But he's not going to."

Knox growled again but didn't move and I felt Audrey's pleasure at knowing that Knox would rather cuddle with her than let the feral creature inside him take over and fight Deacon.

We ate and chatted as the sun sank below the horizon, and it felt right, comfortable. Even Cyrus relaxed and I laughed at a few of Deacon's bad jokes. Whil, whose glow was weak — indicating she'd completely drained her magic saving me — turned in early, and Audrey dozed off in Knox's lap soon after.

We need to talk about what we're returning to, Cyrus said in my head. *Your campaign to show Audrey off at the festival worked on most of the pack, but not all, and Audrey was with you when you were attacked.*

When she *was attacked,* Knox corrected.

Pretty sure the rumor mill will have it twisted around by the time we get back, Deacon replied, and I hated that he was right.

Some of the pack seemed to think so little of Audrey that I doubted it would even occur to them that she had actually been the target. They'd chalk it up to a foreigner attack and not even consider that it could have been a pack member.

Of course, it *hadn't* been a pack member, but it also hadn't been a foreigner, not one I could identify.

I think we might have a bigger problem than the rumor mill, I said, making everyone look at me. *Whatever attacked me and Audrey didn't smell like anything I've ever scented before.*

The closest scent I could compare it to was a grimalkin with its foul, almost rotting scent. Except it hadn't been quite the same, and the thing that had attacked us had fought like a man. It had hidden in the shadows waiting for us and there'd been an intelligence in its attacks that went beyond that of a beast's instincts.

I shuddered. Had the grimalkins gained the ability to shift? The idea seemed impossible, but in a realm where powerful beings leaked their magic into the ground where they slept, anything was possible.

We need Whil looking into whatever it was, I said, even though I knew it was going to be impossible. Without the creature, she had nothing to study, and all we could do was wait for it to make another appearance.

Still doesn't address how we're dealing with Audrey and the pack, Deacon said, knowing as well as I did that Whil couldn't do anything with the current situation.

She's my bonded mate. My fated *mate,* I said. *They're just going to have to get over themselves. You and Cyrus might be more powerful than me, but that doesn't mean I can't defend Audrey or my position in the pack.*

But as soon as I said it, I knew that wasn't what Deacon was really talking about. Not everyone would take a direct path to expressing their dislike for the situation, and that meant Audrey wasn't safe being alone. And trying to convince everyone Audrey and I were fated for each other wasn't going to be easy, either. Velora had already accused Audrey of using magic to trap Knox. She was going to lose her mind when she learned I'd mated Audrey as well.

"Fuck," I hissed. *Velora is going to be a problem.*

She'd been not-so-subtly trying to catch my eye for over a year now, and I'd been trying to keep her at a professional arm's length.

Do you have someone to replace her as beta? Knox asked, jumping straight to the heart of the matter.

Yes, Cyrus replied. *Zondra knows most of what Velora does.*

But it's not that easy, I added, having already had this conversation about replacing Velora with her assistant with Cyrus since she'd been less than welcoming of Audrey. *Her fur is already bristled thinking Audrey is stealing me away. If we release her from her position, we won't be able to keep as close an eye on her and she'll be able to spread rumors.*

More rumors, Deacon corrected. *She hasn't left proof, but I'm pretty sure she's spreading them already and with us gone, I'm sure they've gotten worse.*

Cyrus ran his hands down his face. *She was such a good beta in the beginning.*

Deacon snorted. *She's always had her eye on Bishop and a spot as one of the alpha's mates.*

Well, we all know I'm shit at dealing with situations like this, Cyrus said with a growl of frustration, knowing as we all did that this situation needed to be handled carefully. He couldn't just demote her. *Figure out the best way to approach this,* he said to me, *then tell me what you need me to do.*

I nodded and reached for Audrey's hand, the urge to touch her swelling inside me. I needed to figure out the right way to handle the situation or I'd make everything worse for her.

And while I knew all four of us would fight whoever disagreed with the fact that Audrey was my mate and therefore an alpha of the pack, she'd feel guilty and embarrassed, and I wasn't sure if I could convince her to be angry about it instead. Not yet.

The problem was, I wasn't sure if there *was* a good way out of this.

AUDREY

Six days later, soaked and tired, we returned to Stonehaven. It had started raining just after lunch with the steady stream of a normal storm and not the downpour of a magically enhanced one — thank God. But with no good place to stop on the road between the shelter and Stonehaven, we'd just kept walking.

Well, Cyrus, Deacon, and Knox had kept walking. Whil, Bishop, and I had ridden in the cart... and had been riding in the cart since yesterday morning at Cyrus's command, something I hadn't complained about. I was tired, and my face, while feeling better than when I'd woken after saving Bishop and sealing our bond, was still tender, and my feet hurt.

Thankfully, my mating bond with Bishop hadn't set off another heat, and I hadn't slowed us down or embarrassed myself by jumping my mates or Cyrus and demanding sex for five days straight.

Deacon pulled the cart into the large courtyard where the road led into town, released a heavy sigh, and wiped water out of his eyes. "Home sweet home."

"If you need anything," Whil said, gathering her packs and hopping out of the cart, "ask me in a few days. I plan on sleeping."

"Of course," Cyrus replied scowling at the cart while crossing and uncrossing his arms if he were angry— No, not angry... uncertain?

"Cyrus!" Zavier called out as he rushed across the courtyard.

"You're on duty?" Cyrus asked, his shoulders relaxing as if he knew how to handle *this* situation and was relieved to not have to figure out whatever had been bothering him.

"Just changing shifts with Vida." He jerked his thumb over his shoulder at a woman standing in a security guard box. "I can take care of your cart."

"Thanks," Cyrus replied.

"Also, the delegates from the Mountain and Sea Alliance arrived yesterday. They've probably just started dinner if you wanted to see them tonight."

"Fuck," Bishop hissed as he hopped off the cart and extended a hand to me to help me down. "So much for having a day or two to get organized."

"Alsoooo..." Zavier's gaze jumped to me then jumped away.

Knox growled and jerked closer to me and Bishop, and Zane's eyes flashed wide.

"It's got something to do with Audrey?" Bishop asked.

"There's a rumor going around that Audrey was responsible for Bishop getting hurt."

My throat tightened, a wave of worry and guilt churning in my stomach, and Bishop pulled me into his arms. I couldn't deny it. I *was* responsible for Bishop being poisoned.

"Quinn and I have been spreading the rumor that Audrey and Knox and—" He drew in a sharp breath and squared his shoulders. "And Bishop are fated mates. Quinn thought it best to push the romantic side after you sang *Fated Stars* at the dance." He met Cyrus's gaze head on in a direct challenge to the more powerful alpha. "Quinn just came up with the idea. I'm the one who spread it around. Don't blame her."

"Zavier," Cyrus huffed. "You know I hate rumors."

"I do," Zavier replied, his gaze locking with Cyrus's.

"But I'm glad you and Quinn are working to counteract them."

"And your rumor isn't a rumor," Bishop added, drawing Zavier's attention. "It's true. Just like with Knox, Audrey and I bonded without having to say the vows."

"I knew it!" Zavier fist-punched the air, his gaze flickering to Cyrus so fast I almost missed it.

I wondered if he still had a bet with Quinn that Cyrus was interested in me. Was he hoping Quinn was right and Cyrus would be next? Or was he worried he was going to lose the money he'd won betting on me and Bishop?

"How about you add that Audrey saved Bishop to

your rumor repertoire," Deacon suggested. "Whil did the magic, but if it wasn't for Audrey, he would have died."

"Deacon," I hissed at him. "That's not true."

The huntmaster gave me a dry, *"you didn't really just say that"* look. "What would you say that CPR thing was? He'd stopped breathing and Whil needed more time."

"It's true," Whil added, offering me a soft, exhausted smile. "Without your CPR, I wouldn't have been able to save him."

"He stopped breathing?" Zavier's eyebrows hit his hairline. "I want to know all about it, but Quinn will kill me if I hear it first. I'm already in trouble knowing you two are mate bonded."

"That and it's raining?" Deacon replied, the skin around his eyes crinkling with laughter.

"Fuck! Shit! Ahhh!" Zavier sputtered, realizing we all looked like drowned rats and the rain was still pouring down on us. "I'll take the cart. Go! Go!"

Deacon's smirk deepened. "You're giving your alpha commands now?"

"No, I—

"Stop teasing the kid," Cyrus said, shaking his head at Deacon.

"Not a kid," Zavier mumbled as he hurried to the push bar at the front of the cart.

"No, you're not," Deacon chuckled. "When are you going to mate that sweet little schoolteacher?"

"Deacon!" Cyrus barked with a snap of power that did nothing to diminish Deacon's grin.

"You're horrible," I hissed at the huntmaster as Zavier hurried away with the cart.

"Come on," he groaned. "Everyone can see it but those two."

"And they both *just* turned twenty-one," Bishop said, hefting his pack as Knox took mine and his in one hand and slung them over his shoulder. "They're still young. Give them time."

"They'll realize it soon enough," Whil added, wiping water out of her eyes. "The more you push, the longer they'll resist it."

"True," Deacon sighed. "I remember being an idiot at twenty-one, too."

"You're still an idiot," Cyrus said with a laugh, making me stare at him in surprise.

"Oh my God, did Cyrus just tell a joke?" I whispered to Bishop, knowing Cyrus could still hear me with his wolf-enhanced hearing.

"Yep," Knox replied at full volume.

"Mark it on your calendar," Bishop added, making Cyrus groan and march down the street a little faster.

"Come on," he said over his shoulder as we followed. "You need to get your mate out of the rain and I need to clean up and figure out how to schmooze."

"I'll do all the schmoozing," Bishop said with a sigh. "You can just look important and in charge."

I leaned into Bishop, feeling how tired he was and how much he didn't want to go to dinner tonight and play politics.

"*You*," Cyrus shot back, "are going to Audrey's suite to spend the night. You're both tired, and I'll need you tomorrow when the real schmoozing and politics start. Both of you."

"Both of us?" I squeaked.

This was a trap, a way for Cyrus to make me embarrass myself so he could—

No.

That wasn't how Cyrus did things. He wasn't Merrick.

Still, all those people looking at me, judging me, wondering why the hell I was with the alphas. I wasn't ready for that. I—

Knox's grip on my hand tightened and a wave of support washed through the bond.

"You're mated to two of the three pack alphas," Cyrus said as if he could read my mind. "You're an alpha of this pack, Audrey, and you deserve to be involved in pack business."

"And I want you by my side if you're up for it," Bishop said, his love flooding through our bond, warm and heady. "You're mine and my pack will know it."

"But these talks are important and I don't know your culture let alone your politics." And there'd be so many people staring at me, judging me, wondering why a weakling—

No. Stop thinking that. Stop repeating Merrick and Sterling's poison.

I shoved those horrible thoughts aside, and pride washed through both of Knox's and Bishop's bonds.

"You don't know all our culture or politics," Cyrus said, stepping out of a narrow alley, making me realize we'd stayed to narrow, near-abandoned streets and alleys for Knox — who was still in his human form — and onto the main road leading into Old Town. "But you're very good at being quiet and observing."

"Good idea," Deacon said as if he just realized Cyrus's plan. "Audrey, you're perfect. You won't be able to understand anyone speaking in their native tongue, but you can still see who talks to who and study their body language when they think Cyrus and Bishop aren't paying attention."

"So I'm a spy?" A small glimmer of hope sparked in my chest. I didn't necessarily like the idea of being a spy, but this was a chance to prove my usefulness to the pack.

"You're an observer," Cyrus corrected, "and only if you want to."

"I do. I'll do it." All those years of being beaten into submission and of trying to stay small and unnoticed might actually become good for something.

AUDREY

We separated when we reached the Residence, Cyrus and Deacon entering through the front door, Whil heading across the grounds to the cottage, and Bishop, Knox, and I walking around the castle to my suite's French doors. We were already soaked so a few more minutes in the rain wouldn't hurt us, and I wasn't ready to leave Knox just yet or have Bishop taken away on pack business by someone, especially not Velora

The mattress that had been set on the small patio when Bishop had been poisoned so Knox could stay with him was gone, but Knox didn't hesitate — there barely a flicker of fear in our bond — as he followed me and Bishop inside.

"Let's get you cleaned up and warm," Bishop said, a hint of seduction in his voice but not enough to overcome my exhaustion or the exhaustion I knew he was feeling.

Even after seven days and having shifted every day to

speed up his recovery, he still didn't have the stamina he used to have, and I feared he'd never get it back.

All because he'd protected me.

And while I could feel in our bond that he didn't blame me and would do it again if it meant protecting me, I still felt guilty.

"She's tired," Knox said, his voice a low growl as he and Bishop ushered me into the bathroom.

"Yeah," I mumbled, not resisting them when they positioned me in front of the shower.

"You'll be happier after you sleep." Knox turned on the taps, the sudden *shush* of water startling me as if I'd dozed off for a second.

"I don't like where your thoughts go when you're tired," Bishop said, grabbing the hem of my shirt and peeling the almost see-through fabric up my torso.

Jeez, I must have been tired if I hadn't even noticed that my thin shirt clung to my chest doing nothing to hide the fact my nipples were pebbled from the chilly rain and the fabric hugged the curve of my breasts like a second skin.

"Audrey, whatever you're worried about, we'll face it together. The three of us," he said.

Knox grunted in agreement, and Bishop cupped my cheeks with his palms, urging me to look at him.

The warm endless night of his gaze captured mine, suspending me with the certainty of his love, and I floated among brilliant green stars. In his eyes, I was precious and desired. Neither Bishop nor Knox blamed me for what had happened, something I already knew. But it was harder to fight my demons when I was tired. When all three of us were tired.

I pushed love through the bonds, hoping to give them strength, but Knox growled and a snap of his power broke my concentration.

"But I—" I protested. I wanted to help them, *needed* to help them.

"It's our turn, mate," Knox huffed. "You held me together the whole walk to the pool when you were suffering too—"

"And sent me support to keep my strength up the whole walk back," Bishop finished. "Yeah, we're all tired. But you're exhausted, Audrey, and you can't even see it."

"And when you're exhausted," Knox said, "the shit those assholes fed you while you were growing up gets louder.

"Are you listening to my thoughts now?" I asked. It was rude to eavesdrop on people's thoughts and no shifter that I knew about could do it consistently — although it wouldn't surprise me if Knox, Bishop, and Cyrus could.

"Don't need to," Knox huffed as he knelt in front of me and pulled down my pants. "It's so obvious, even I can figure it out."

"Hey," I huffed back. "Don't insult my mate."

He rolled his eyes at me, grabbed my hips, and buried his nose in my curls.

You're mate still can't believe he's yours, he said in my

head. *And I'll spend the rest of my life worshiping you to make amends for hurting you in the beginning.*

"You *were* an asshole," Bishop chuckled. He pressed his lips against mine, his tongue teasing the seam of my mouth, asking for entrance.

I opened and let him in for a long, languid kiss full of tongue, while Knox licked and sucked just as slowly at my entrance.

The fire of need grew slow and steady, building and building until rolling over me. It wasn't the biggest orgasm either of my guys had ever given me, but it was still perfect. Hot and flowing, dragging tension I hadn't noticed I had from my body.

It was exactly what I needed to let go of the worry and adrenaline that I'd clung to in order to stay strong for them.

"That's it," Bishop purred, and together he and Knox drew me into the shower, cleaning me with loving and gentle attention.

They kept me relaxed, not giving my mind a chance to return to my worries with soft, flesh against flesh teasing but not building my desire any tighter.

It was perfect. All of us were too tired for much more, and after I was clean and bundled in a warm fluffy towel, I climbed into bed sandwiched between them.

At some point in the night, Knox left, his claustrophobia forcing him outside. He lasted longer than he said he could and had only just started to get uncomfortable, suggesting maybe, with love and patience, his time indoors could be extended.

I drifted back asleep, my heart warm with their bonds, and when I woke with brilliant morning sunlight streaming through the windows, the warmth was still there.

My lips curled into a soft lazy smile. I lay in my mate's arms, my back pressed against a firm, muscular chest, safe and secure and loved.

And then I realized who held me, and my smile grew into a goofy grin.

Knox.

He'd come back to bed.

"Bishop had to take care of pack business before breakfast," Knox rumbled in my ear, his hot breath washing over the back of my neck.

"So you thought you'd keep me warm?" I turned in his arms and nuzzled my nose into the crook of his neck, breathing in his rich wood smoke scent.

"Always. I came back an hour and a half before Bishop had to leave," he said and I couldn't even feel a hint of anxiety from him.

"Thank you."

He huffed his acknowledgment, the love in the bond saying more than words, and brushed his lips against mine with the beginning of a kiss, but stopped and groaned a second later.

"Asshole," he hissed, rolling away from me onto his back. "Bishop says breakfast will be here in five. He wants me to wake you, ensure you've eaten and changed into the dress he's sending with our meal, and have you outside the Residence's front doors in twenty minutes."

"We could still..." I said, sliding my hand down his chest.

But he grabbed my wrist before I could reach his cock. "You can't be late and you can't look recently fucked. Cyrus and Bishop are taking the alliance members on a tour of the city."

And the whole point of me being there was to not draw attention to myself, something that would definitely happen if I was late.

"Bishop promises some of that later," Knox said with a wolfish smile sending heat rushing to my core. "He's going to have to wait his turn."

AUDREY

THE DRESS WAS A BEAUTIFUL EMERALD GREEN, THE SAME shade as the flecks in Bishop's and Knox's eyes with flowers embroidered on the bodice in golden thread.

It was a similar design to the dresses that were popular in the pack with a tie securing it around my neck and another mid-back to give it shape. But instead of being completely backless, the fabric tucked around me at the middle of my back, hiding two of the four large puncture-wound scars marring my skin and the tie around my neck was also slightly different. It was thinner than the usual design, revealing more of my neck and shoulders, and ensured both Knox's and Bishop's mating marks were clearly visible.

No one would be able to question if I was mated to them with the very permanent and uncommon bite-mark scars out in the open. And while I was thrilled at the idea that my mates weren't embarrassed by me and wanted their whole pack to know I belonged to them, it also made me nervous. Not everyone would like that I mate bonded with Bishop, and I needed to be wary and on my best behavior to avoid causing problems.

"Stay close to Bishop or Cyrus," Knox said, his gaze locked on his mating mark as lust oozed like lava through our bond. "I'll keep an eye on you as best I can, but part of the tour involves the market and there are too many people there."

"I'll stay close." And I wouldn't cause a scene. Although I knew that wasn't what Knox was worried about.

Whoever had attacked me and Bishop was still out there. I doubted they'd outright attack me while surrounded by dozens of witnesses, but those same people could act as cover for a secret attack, like a nick with one of his poisoned claws. It would be as easy as someone bumping into me.

A shiver rolled down my spine and Knox pulled me into a tight hug.

"I won't let anything happen to you."

"I know," I said against his chest as I nuzzled closer and drew in a breath heavy with comforting wood smoke. "I trust you."

"Good. Now go before I rip this dress off you and fuck you senseless."

A wave of need slammed into me and I groaned as I stepped out of his embrace.

"When this is done..." he promised.

He yanked off his shirt, dropped his pants, and shifted into his enormous black wolf.

I bit back another groan. This tour couldn't end fast enough.

You coming, Audrey? Bishop asked in my head, sending more need rushing through me. *The tour is about to start.*

Oh, she'll be coming. Tonight, Knox replied, making Bishop groan and me shiver in anticipation.

"Stop with the sex comments. I'm going to smell like I'm in heat again," I huffed, trying to think of ice-cold showers.

Only the other members of our pack, the gryphons, and the Dedearc will notice, Knox replied.

"That's two-thirds of the tour group."

Knox chuffed with wolfy laughter. *More like half. There's a human kingdom and a human independent state in the Alliance.*

"Still doesn't make me feel better."

But the embarrassment of smelling like I needed sex cooled some of my desires, and I hurried out onto my patio before either of my mates could work me up again.

Knox followed beside me until we reached the edge of the Residence and our next turn would make us visible to whoever stood in the front courtyard. He sent a wave of love and confidence into the bond and stepped out of sight behind a hedgerow.

I squared my shoulders determined to appear confident despite the voice from my past insisting that I didn't belong and rounded the corner.

Close to three dozen people gathered in the center of the courtyard near the fountain with the two enormous wolves on either side of a woman pouring water from a large urn.

As Knox said, half of them were human with varying degrees of sun-kissed skin, from golden tan to rich dark brown, and three-quarters of them were men. About half of the men wore military style uniforms and by the looks of them, represented two different militaries. The other men wore clean, tailored clothes while none of the human women wore military uniforms. They all wore dresses, some elaborate and some quite plain.

Beside them were two men and five women who looked human — the same height and build as the others — but they weren't. They gave off a predatory, shifter vibe that I didn't recognize and wore clothing similar to our pack's clothing. They had to be the gryphons, a type of shifter everyone in my realm thought was just legend like all the other fairy tale shifters: dragons, hydra, unicorns, and elementals.

To the right of them, a few steps away from the humans, were six enormous lizard-like people. The Dedearc.

I'd seen a few of them the last time I'd visited the market and hadn't wanted to stare, so I hadn't gotten a good look at them. But now, standing a good fifty feet away, I had a chance to study their unique features.

They reminded me of some of the demons I'd seen on TV. They had human-shaped bodies that were covered in scales — black or dark red or blue on their back and shifting to cream or white on their front. They had a lizard-like tail and a reptile-like head, and a few of them had short horns at their temples like incubi or succubi, reinforcing my suspicion that they were a type of demon or at least had demon ancestors.

They all wore the same loose clothing made from a shimmering silky fabric that was cut to accommodate their tail but didn't give me a hint to their gender. Of course, for all I knew, their species might not have a gender.

Lucius and another wolf shifter, a woman I didn't recognize, talked with the shortest of the Dedearcs who still stood half a head taller than him, which meant all the Dedearc were at least a head — and a few even head and shoulders — taller than the humans and gryphons, while Bishop talked to a Dedearc a head taller than him and two of the humans in military uniform.

Nearby, Deacon talked with three human men wearing fancier clothes. Their complexion was fairer than the other humans and their facial features sharper and narrower. All three of them would have been handsome if they hadn't been giving me an ever-so-slightly creepy vibe.

Even from where I stood at the edge of the Residence, I could sense — either from their body language or from whatever small wolf instinct I had — that they didn't belong with any of the other humans and were trying too hard to be nice to everyone.

Sterling had played that game with me too many times when I'd first moved into his house, and I'd learned my lesson not to trust anyone who's too friendly or too helpful. They wanted something. And the moment they didn't get what they wanted, their fake friendliness vanished and I'd be punished.

The Residence's front doors opened, and Cyrus walked out, drawing everyone's attention. His arrival probably marked the beginning of the tour, so I hurried toward the group.

I got halfway before Velora stepped out from the shade of a tree and grabbed my wrist.

"Where do you think you're going?" she hissed. "You don't belong here."

I tried to wrench free of her grip, but with her shifter enhanced strength, I didn't stand a chance.

"You go right back to that suite you don't deserve and stay there until the Alliance meeting is over."

My instincts to shrink in on myself and look at my feet in submission screamed at me, and I fought with everything I had to keep my head up. "Let me go."

"Not until you're where you belong."

She yanked on my arm, making me stumble, and marched back the way I'd come, not waiting for me to catch my balance.

"Velora," Bishop snapped from behind us, his voice quiet, low enough that the Alliance delegates wouldn't hear, but edged with steel.

"Bishop," she purred. She spun around, jerking me off

balance again, and gave him a heated look. She even battered her eyelashes at him as if that would make her more attractive.

A growl bubbled in my throat. She was trying to take what was mine and that ferociousness trapped deep inside me didn't like that. Not. One. Bit.

But before I could foolishly attack her, Bishop snarled, her attempt at flirting hardening his expression and making my ferociousness preen with satisfaction.

"What are you doing with my mate?" he ground out.

"Your mate?" Velora hissed, her eyes flashing wide.

She jerked her attention back to me, her gaze jumping from one mating mark on my shoulder to the other and back again.

Something ugly passed across her expression then disappeared as she turned back to him, returning to overly flirty. "Congratulations, Bishop. You should have told me you'd picked your first mate."

"My *only* mate," he replied, making my soul sing with pride and pleasure while the cautious part of me cringed.

I didn't want Bishop to lead Velora or anyone else on, but there was no wiggle room in his declaration. There was no reason for her to pretend to be nice to me anymore.

"She's mated to two of the pack's alphas." Bishop held his hand out to me and I took it. He tucked me against his side, reinforcing his claim on me. "She belongs at our side, especially during political events."

"Of course, alpha." Velora dipped her head in submission but managed to glare at me through her lashes. "I'll make sure she has a place at the alpha's table at dinner tonight."

"It's already taken care of. Come on, Audrey," he said, and he turned his back on Velora. "The tour has already started. We need to catch up before we fall behind."

We hurried after the group of delegates as they stepped through the open gate separating the Residence from Old Town. I kept my focus ahead of me, knowing Velora was trying to burn a hole in the back of my head.

I didn't want another confrontation with her, especially without Bishop, Knox, or Cyrus nearby, and I could only pray with Bishop claiming me and not leaving room for doubt, she'd finally move on.

But I'd never been so lucky before and I doubted my luck would improve now.

AUDREY

THE TOUR MARCHED DOWN THE MAIN ROAD THROUGH OLD Town and into the newer part of Stonehaven. Cyrus took the lead and talked with the King of Lais, His Majesty King Gower, who was a tall, broad-shoulder man in a crisp military uniform.

The king would have looked imposing if he hadn't been walking between Cyrus — who was taller and broader — and Pimryl, the imposing female leader of Ocasha, a Dedearc colony on the coast north of the Kingdom of Lais who stood a head and a half taller than him.

Just behind Pimryl's shoulder walked the smallest Dedearc of the Dedearc representatives who I was told was the only male in the party. He repeated everything Cyrus and King Gower said to Pimryl in a soft, unobtrusive voice.

"This is our school," Cyrus announced, pointing to

the large, three-story building where I'd attended Nova's first aid class. "It's mandatory for all pups when they turn five to attend the school for ten years."

"Starting at age five, all children must attend school for ten years," the male Dedearc repeated.

Pimryl nodded, keeping her attention on Cyrus and the school. "No wonder your warriors are so tenacious. You start training them at such a young age."

"It's impressive that you train your warriors for so long," the male Dedearc said to Cyrus even though Cyrus kept looking at Pimryl.

"Not just warriors," Cyrus replied, leading the group back to the main road and continuing our slow journey to the market where we were going to stop for lunch. "Scientists, engineers, artists, musicians, writers, philosophers. The first six years include every subject. After that, pups can pick a specialization or not. They can also voluntarily study for more than ten years."

"We have a similar system," Representative Folmar said. She was a stocky, middle-aged woman and the leader of the gryphons shifters.

The male Dedearc repeated what both Cyrus and Folmar said, and Pimryl nodded. It was as if she didn't understand what the others were saying.

I turned my attention to the other group of humans from the Independent State of Ciliran and the three merchants who were hoping to sell their grimalkin killing weapons to the Alliance.

Jundar, who was the representative from Ciliran and

the Speaker of the Alliance — kind of like the Speaker of the House — had a young woman repeating everything, while the merchants didn't. But there were times when the merchants said something to each other and no one seemed to understand them.

Well, shit, I mentally huffed at myself as realization hit me so hard Knox sent worry through our bond and Bishop jerked his attention away from what he'd been saying to Folmar to look at me.

What? Bishop asked in my head, drawing us to the side of the group as Lucius pointed out another building of interest.

"Those two—" I whispered, pointing at the male Dedearc and the human who repeated everything. "They're translators, aren't they."

Bishop frowned. "It's taken you this long to figure that out? They're obviously speaking different languages."

"Not to me."

My thoughts lurched to the memory of being at the death god's altar and Bishop reciting the spell to break my bond with Knox. He'd read the spell off a piece of paper but it had been as if he'd forgotten how to speak. His pronunciation had become weird and the words had been broken into syllables.

I rolled my eyes at myself. "What language was the spell to break my bond in?"

"An ancient dialect. Whil assured me my pronunciation was good, but I've wondered if I was the one who screwed up the spell."

"If that's what happened, I'm glad you did screw it up," I said, leaning into him. As much as Knox and I'd had a rocky start, I knew in my soul that being mating to him, just like being mated to Bishop, was the way it was supposed to be.

"Why the questions?" he asked.

"Because I understood what you said for the spell, and I understand what Pimryl and Jundar are saying before their translators translate for them. It's all English to me."

Bishop's eyes widened. "The magic that helps you understand us, lets you understand every language?"

"Looks like," I replied as we slowed to walk behind the group of delegates and their aides.

Cyrus, you need to know this, Bishop said with his shifter telepathy.

Cyrus gave an ever-so-slight nod and gestured for Lucius to explain the next point of interest.

What? Cyrus asked.

Audrey doesn't need a translator.

Because of the magic that lets her understand us? Cyrus asked, instantly jumping to the same conclusion Bishop had.

Exactly, Bishop replied.

Stay near the middle of the group, Cyrus commanded without any additional questions or hesitation, sending a strange sensation rushing through my chest.

He trusted me. He had no doubt that I was telling the

truth, and it felt weird to not have to submit to questions and criticisms and disbelief.

When the tour is done, Cyrus said, *you can tell me if you overheard anything that we should be worried about.*

Especially from the merchants, Bishop added, his agreement with Cyrus's order to double down on my spying assignment and the confidence that I could do it flooding through our bond. *I've got a bad feeling about them.*

Me, too, Cyrus confessed before turning to Folmar and answering her question without missing a beat, giving no indication that he'd just had a mental conversation with us.

Then Cyrus stopped in front of a long, squat building on the corner of the main street and a narrower one and explained that it was Stonehaven's public works building, giving me and Bishop a chance to ease into the center of the group.

Jundar, the representative from Ciliran, asked a question that was word for word translated by the young woman standing slightly behind him, and Bishop answered.

"So there's no private construction?" One of the merchants asked. He was a lanky man who was almost as tall as Bishop but half of Bishop's weight and wore a silky robe with thick, complicated embroidery at the neck, cuffs, and hem.

"What I really want to see is their armory," another merchant with a similar build in a similar robe replied.

The third merchant, the shortest and stockiest of the

group, nodded to Merchant Two but no one else reacted, and Jundar's translator didn't repeat his words.

One of the Ciliran men in military uniform gave the merchants a quick glance before jerking his attention forward and following the people in front of him as Cyrus turned off the main road, heading to the market.

"You can glare at them all you like," the soldier beside him said, his voice low enough that the human merchants wouldn't have heard him, but all the shifters — and me, who was right behind him — still could.

"I don't like them," he replied. "If their weapons are as powerful as they say, we have no choice but to buy them at the price they're selling them at. We can't even negotiate. If we do, they'll either sell them to a hostile country or outright attack us."

"That's why the whole Alliance has twice as many soldiers as usual for this meeting."

I frowned. It looked like Cyrus, Bishop, and I weren't the only ones who had bad feelings about the merchants.

"Trying to learn Cilirinian?" A broad-shouldered gryphon shifter about my age asked.

Ferocious feralness radiated off him, and I could sense an enormous alpha power within him ... which was impossible. I should have only been able to sense a wolf's level of alpha power, not that of another shifter.

"My mother's been trying to learn it for years," he said, jerking his chin toward Folmar who was deep in conversation with Cyrus and Pimryl. "I'm told the trick is to listen to the pitch as well as the words." He flashed me a chagrined smile as we strolled into the heart of the market, people making way for our larger group. "But I'm tone-deaf, so I really can't say."

I had no idea how to respond to him. I couldn't tell him I'd been eavesdropping. That would ruin my advantage over everyone who spoke a different language.

"Does it frustrate you?" I finally asked after too long a pause, making him frown. "Being tone-deaf, I mean."

"You have no idea," he said with a groan and a self-deprecating smile. "One-third of our courtship rituals involve singing."

"What are the other two-thirds?" I asked.

"Displaying our feathers and a little primal chasing." He dropped his voice into a conspiratorial whisper. "Thank the Sisters they gave me beautiful feathers and a love for the hunt, or my mother would have completely given up on me."

His expression soured with his last words, and I opened my mouth to ask him about what he meant when a terrified scream tore through the mix of voices from the market.

My pulse lurched.

Oh, no. Please, no.

Then a wave of panicked people rushed our way followed by six enormous grimalkins.

Don't miss the next book in the series!

Wolf Devoted
Ensnared by the Pack: Book Six

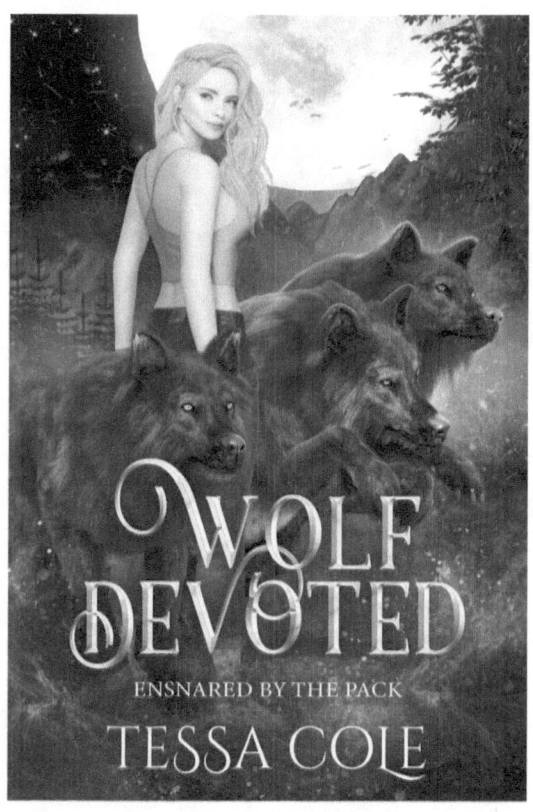

OTHER BOOKS BY TESSA COLE

NEPHILIM'S DESTINY

Destined Shadows, prequel story

Destined Darkness, book 1

Destined Blood, book 2

Destined Fire, book 3

Destined Storm, book 4

Destined Radiance, book 5

ANGEL'S FATE

Fated Bonds, book 1

Fated Winter, book 2

Fated Fear, book 3

Fated Despair, book 4

Fated Resolve, book 5

Fated Heart, book 6

ENSNARED BY THE PACK

Wolf Deceived, book 1

Wolf Denied, book 2

Wolf Desired, book 3

Wolf Distressed, book 4

Wolf Decided, book 5

Wolf Devoted, book 6

THE GRECIAN GODDESS TRILOGY

Kiss of the Goddess, book 1

Power of the Goddess, book 2

Bonds of the Goddess, book 3